The Desert

Middle East Literature in Translation
Michael Beard and Adnan Haydar, *Series Editors*

Other titles from Middle East Literature in Translation

Arabs and the Art of Storytelling: A Strange Familiarity
Abdelfattah Kilito; Mbarek Sryfi and Eric Sellin, trans.

Chronicles of Majnun Layla and Selected Poems
Qassim Haddad

The Emperor Tea Garden
Nazlı Eray; Robert Finn, trans.

Monarch of the Square: An Anthology of Muhammad Zafzaf's Short Stories
Mbarek Sryfi and Roger Allen, trans.

My Torturess
Bensalem Himmich; Roger Allen, trans.

The Pistachio Seller
Reem Bassiouney; Osman Nusairi, trans.

A Sleepless Eye: Aphorisms from the Sahara
Ibrahim al-Koni; Roger Allen, trans.

The Story of Joseph: A Fourteenth-Century Turkish Morality Play by Sheyyad Hamza
Bill Hickman, trans.

The Desert

Or, the Life *and* Adventures of Jubair Wali al-Mammi

Albert Memmi

Translated from the French by
Judith Roumani

Syracuse University Press

First published as *Le Désert, ou la Vie et les Aventures de Jubaïr Ouali El-Mammi*, Paris, Editions Gallimard, 1977, 1989. English translation copyright Judith Roumani 1980, 2008.

The translator's introduction appeared in an earlier version in *Philological Quarterly* 61, no. 3 (Spring 1982). With thanks to the editors of *Philological Quarterly* for permission to republish in revised and updated form. One chapter of the translation, "Younous," since revised, appeared in *Jewish Frontier* 50, no. 4 (April 1983). Thanks also to Eleanor Levieux and Penguin Random House for permission to use the epigraph from *The Scorpion*.

Syracuse University Press
Syracuse, New York 13244-5290

First Edition 2015
15 16 17 18 19 20 6 5 4 3 2 1

∞ The paper used in this publication meets the minimum requirements of the American National Standard for Information Sciences—Permanence of Paper for Printed Library Materials, ANSI Z39.48-1992.

For a listing of books published and distributed by Syracuse University Press, visit www.SyracuseUniversityPress.syr.edu.

ISBN: 978-0-8156-1055-7 (paperback) 978-0-8156-5335-6 (e-book)

Library of Congress Cataloging-in-Publication Data

Memmi, Albert.
[Désert. English]
The desert : or, The life and adventures of Jubair Wali al-Mammi / Albert Memmi ; translated from the French by Judith Roumani. — First edition.
pages cm. — (Middle East literature in translation)
ISBN 978-0-8156-1055-7 (pbk. : alk. paper) — ISBN 978-0-8156-5335-6 (e-book)
I. Roumani, Judith, translator. II. Title. III. Title: Life and adventures of Jubair Wali al-Mammi.
PQ2625.E39D413 2015
843'.914—dc23 2015025575

Manufactured in the United States of America

A Maïra, sorcière bénéfique
(To Maira, the good witch)

The first certain indication of our presence here . . . is found in the Arab historian El-Milli. In his Arab-Berber Chronicles, he lists one El-Mammi among the companions of the famous Judeo-Berber Queen Cahena.

—*The Scorpion*, Albert Memmi (trans. Eleanor Levieux [New York: Grossman, 1971], 18).

I don't know whether our ancestor eventually became king, but I do know that I owe my wisdom to him. In telling you the story of his life, so that you can tell it to your children, I am repaying an enormous debt at minimal cost.

—Uncle Makhlouf

Contents

Illustrations

Translator's Introduction

The Desert *as Folktale, Chronicle, and Biography*

The Desert, Albert Memmi's fourth novel, first published in 1977, attempts through fiction to reintegrate a traditional civilization with modernity. Drawing on the techniques of North African oral literature and Oriental genres, Memmi proposes a value system and world view which consciously echo, with modern overtones, medieval North African philosophy. The structure and technique of the novel transform Memmi's nostalgic evocation of his cultural roots into a cyclical vision of history and a view of how the wise man relates to the community.

Despite having published three previous novels, Memmi has been known less as a novelist than as an *engagé* political sociologist/

An earlier version of this essay was previously published in *Philological Quarterly* 61, no. 2 (Spring 1982), 193–207, under the title "Memmi's Introduction to History: *Le Désert* as Folktale, Chronicle and Biography." With thanks to the editors of *Philological Quarterly* for permission to republish in revised and updated form. Other studies of the novel are Isaac Yetiv, "Du *Scorpion* au *Désert*: Albert Memmi Revisited," *Studies in Twentieth-Century Literature* 7, no. 1 (1982): 77–82; ibid., "From Ethnocentrism to Humanism: Albert Memmi's *Le Désert*," *International Fiction Review* 16, no. 2 (1989): 128–31; Dalia Kandiyoti, "The Possibilities of History: *The Desert* and North African Jewish Identity," *European Legacy* 1, no. 4 (1996): 1452–58; and Lia Nicole Brozgal's "Blindness, the Visual, and Ekphrastic Impulses: Albert Memmi Colours in the Lines," *French Studies* 64, no. 3 (2010): 317–28 (pp. 324–25 discuss the illustrations). See also Afifa and Samir Marzouki, *Individu et communautés dans l'oeuvre littéraire d'Albert Memmi* (Paris: L'Harmattan, 2010), 15–16, and chapter 8.

philosopher writing about colonized peoples and minorities in general.[1] *The Desert* commands attention because it helped to correct this notion of his work, current at the time. Memmi expressed such a desire in an interview, saying that events and circumstances, "m'ont fait devenir également un écrivain de combat, plus connu ainsi que comme romancier, ce que je regrette un peu. . . . J'espère revenir définitivement au roman, à la fiction."[2] (caused me to also become a fighting writer, better known for that than for being a novelist, which I somewhat regret . . . I hope to return once and for all to the novel, to fiction.)

In *The Desert: Or, the Life and Adventures of Jubair Wali al-Mammi*,[3] Memmi gives his imagination freer rein than before. He applies himself fully as an artist (or, as he prefers to say, a traditional craftsman) to creating an imaginative artifact. Through *The Desert* Memmi also tries to open up a new field for the North African novel: going beyond autobiography or contemporary problems, he sets out to embody the historical imagination. One of his strategies in *The Desert* is to approach traditional genres which celebrate the exploits of peoples and their legendary heroes.

Memmi's earlier novels are albums of personal snapshots taken en route to his partial Westernization. *The Pillar of Salt* and *Strangers*[4]

1. For example, Albert Memmi, *Portrait du colonisé: Précédé de Portrait du colonisateur*, pref. Jean-Paul Sartre (1957); rev. ed. Gallimard, 2003, this being the most recent of many individual editions; and *L'Homme dominé* (Paris: Gallimard, 1968, Payot 1973); trans. as *Dominated Man* (New York: Orion, 1968). A volume bringing together all the Portraits has recently been published in Paris, edited by Guy Dugas: *Albert Memmi. Portraits* (Paris: CNRS editions, 2015).

2. Albert Memmi, *La Terre intérieure: Entretien avec Victor Malka* (Paris: Gallimard, 1976), 10.

3. Albert Memmi, *Le Désert ou La Vie et les aventures de Jubaïr Ouali el-Mammi* (Paris: Gallimard, 1977; Gallimard Folio, 1989). Subsequent references are to the 1977 edition.

4. Albert Memmi, *La Statue de sel*, 1953; rev. ed. pref. Albert Camus (1955; Paris: Gallimard, 1966); rev. ed. in English, trans. Edouard Roditi, *The Pillar of Salt*, 1955 (Boston: Beacon, 1992); *Agar*, 1955, and many subsequent editions,

are autobiographical novels that dramatize, with less technical elaboration, fictional events from Memmi's childhood and youth.[5] Their main interest lies in their sincere portrayal of the alienation of an individual caught between conflicting cultures. *The Scorpion*[6] elaborates on this autobiographical theme; it combines fictional letters, a diary, and drafts for a novel, showing considerable literary sophistication, and portrays cultural problems in Tunisia after independence.

Memmi approaches history initially through a rediscovery of family origins. His early novels examined his family and the personalities composing it. *The Scorpion* introduced family history through an ancient Punic/Carthaginian coin discovered near Tunis, with the family name engraved on it. This coin is one of the objects which are the key to Memmi's literary *patrie.* Like Proust's madeleines, certain objects, tastes, and smells open the way to his "*petite patrie portative*,"[7] his "*terre intérieure.*" Memmi's evocation in *The Scorpion* of his family's history, together with a few anecdotes about life in an ancient kingdom, thus point toward the later inspiration of *The Desert.*

---

including most recently Tunis: Cérès Editions, 2007, in English trans. Brian Rhys, *Strangers* (New York: Orion, 1960).

5. For Memmi's view of growing up in a colonized society, see his recent essay, "L'Enfance d'un minoritaire," trans. Ralph Tarica as "Growing Up as a Minority Child," part of "An Albert Memmi Anthology," *Sephardic Horizons* 1, no. 2 (Spring 2011), http://sephardichorizons.org.

6. Albert Memmi, *Le Scorpion ou la Confession imaginaire* (Paris: Gallimard, 1969); trans. Eleanor Levieux, *The Scorpion: Or, the Imaginary Confession* (New York: Grossman, 1971).

7. *Le Scorpion*, 242–43; the novelist Emile expresses the idea: "Avec cela je peux, je veux aller au bout du monde; chaque partie de moi-même à volonté reconstituée. Petite patrie portative." English translation, 204: "With that I can go—I would like to go to the end of the world; each part of myself reconstituted at will. A little portable homeland."

Memmi himself has a similar collection of objects provoking memory through the senses (pepper, a set of spices, a piece of leather, different kinds of amber) near his work table. It includes a photograph of the Punic/Carthaginian coin, which is in the Bardo Museum in Tunis.

Other passages in *The Scorpion* discuss whether Memmi is an indigenous Berber name or that of a family originating in Italy. The former hypothesis is supported thus: "La première mention sure de notre presence ici . . . se trouve chez l'historien arabe El-Milli qui, dans ses *Chroniques arabo-berbères*, cite parmi les compagnons de la Cahéna, la fameuse reine judéo-berbère, un certain El-Mammi."[8] (The first certain indication of our presence here . . . is found in the Arab historian El-Milli. In his Arab-Berber Chronicles, he lists one El-Mammi among the companions of the famous Judeo-Berber queen Cahena.) (Trans. Levieux, 18).

The Desert takes up the story of this earliest ancestor (citing a transparently fabricated source) and purports in its preface to be the promised continuation of the chronicles of Le Royaume du Dedans, the Kingdom of Within. The narrator, the long-exiled prince of the kingdom, now defeated by Tamerlane,[9] offers his tale in response to an inquiry from the conqueror, holding court in Damascus, as to how his own realms might be saved from the same fate. The aging al-Mammi sees his duty to respond as an opportunity to spin a story, which happens to be an account of his own adventures. Al-Mammi implies that, through wise governance of his realms and impulses, Tamerlane may prevent his own empire from falling to another conqueror in turn. *The Desert* thus resembles Memmi's earlier novels in taking the form of a fictional autobiography.[10] But the relation between actual events and

8. *Le Scorpion*, 25. This information that Memmi kindly provided in an interview (conducted by Jacques Roumani, in Paris, on December 4, 1977) is important for an understanding of his imaginative transformation of the stuff of his upbringing into a formally constructed novel.

9. In reality, Tamerlane never reached as far as North Africa, and certainly not southern Morocco, where al-Mammi's kingdom is situated (see map).

10. The new term for this in literary criticism is *autofiction* and, for writing by a Jewish author, *autojudeography*. See Thomas Nolden, "A la recherche du judaïsme perdu: Contemporary Jewish Writing in France," in *Contemporary Jewish Writing in Europe: A Guide*, ed. Vivian Liska and Thomas Nolden (Bloomington: Indiana Univ. Press, 2008), 118–38, esp. 125–26. According to Nolden, the term was invented by Robert Ouaknine.

fiction is richer and more complicated here than in any of his earlier novels. The key to Memmi's aesthetic in *The Desert* seems to lie in the use of history.

Memmi explains his attitude to chronicled history as follows: "Les faits historiques ne me servent pas tellement come faits mais comme détonateurs, catalyseurs." (I use historical facts not so much as facts, but rather as detonators, catalyzers.) From the earliest pages, the novelist—or rather, fictional narrator—appears to take pains to fix the setting in time and place for readers not familiar with it: "dans l'extrême nord du Touat, entre Tamentit et Sbe-Guerrara, il a existé un petit royaume indépendant . . ." (11–12 and 13–14 in the French). (In the Gurara, in the extreme north of the Touat region between Tamentit and Sba-Gerara, there existed a small independent kingdom) (1, and map on 4, with a map of the region in southern Morocco). This quotation is lifted almost directly from a historical study, but the information is misleading as "historical fact": like Borges's ironic literary scholarship, these references are reliable mainly as landmarks in the world of the novelist's imagination. Memmi has thoroughly read in available sources on a small Jewish kingdom that existed in that area,[11] but his novel derives equally from Muslim and Jewish history. The original source of information, and the one to which all subsequent scholars refer, is in fact the work of the Muslim historian of the fifteenth century, Ibn Khaldun.[12]

11. Memmi stated in the interview, "J'ai fait le maximum de lectures possible . . ." They may include Haim Hirschberg, *A History of the Jews in North Africa* (1965; trans. Leiden: Brill, 1974); Nahum Slouschz, *Travels in North Africa* (Philadelphia: Jewish Publication Society, 1927); André Chouraqui, *Marche vers l'Occident: Les Juifs d'Afrique du Nord* (Paris: Presses universitaires, 1952), esp. 34 trans. as *Between East and West: A History of the Jews of North Africa* (Philadelphia: Jewish Publication Society, 1968), 19. This seems to be the source for "Ce qu'en disent les historiens" *Le Désert*, 11–12. Memmi would not have been aware, in the mid-1970s, of Jacob Oliel's research, as his first book on the subject was not published until 1994. See Jacob Oliel, *Les Juifs au Sahara: le Touat au Moyen Age* (Paris: CNRS, 1994).

12. Memmi may have referred to the French translation, *Histoire des Berbères et des dynasties musulmanes de l'Afrique septentrionale*, 2 vols., trans. W. M. de Slane

The life of Ibn Khaldun also provided the pattern for the novel's hero. The fictional al-Mammi, courtier, politician, and chronicler of his times, is based fairly closely on the historical Ibn Khaldun, who met Tamerlane in 1401.[13] But the novel establishes a fictional connection between the destruction of the kingdom and al-Mammi's encounter with Tamerlane in 1401, which has no parallel in the case of Ibn Khaldun:

> C'est en 1392, après un assaut decisive de Tamerlan, suivi d'un massacre à peu près complet de la population, que le Royaume-du-Dedans cessa d'exister. Huit ans après, en 1400 exactement, dans la ville de Damas, mise à sac à son tour par le meme conquérant, El-Mammi présentait ses hommages au vainqueur. (12)

> (It was in 1392, after a decisive assault by Tamerlane, followed by an almost total massacre of the population, that the Kingdom of Within ceased to exist. Eight years later, in 1400 to be exact, in the city of Damascus which had been sacked in turn by the same conqueror, al-Mammi was paying obeisance to the victor.) (1–2)

(1847–51; rpt. Paris: Guithner, 1968). A recent study of Ibn Khaldun emphasizes the centrality of his autobiography to his *Muqaddima*. Allen Fromherz writes: "As well as an extraordinary work of history and social philosophy, the *Muqaddima* is Ibn Khaldun explaining himself to himself." See Allen Fromherz, "Ibn Khaldun, *'Asabiyya* and Legitimacy," in *The Articulation of Power in Medieval Iberia*, ed. Amira Bennison (Oxford: Oxford Univ. Press and the British Academy, 2014), 47–57, esp. 54.b The source of al-Mammi's first name is likely a twelfth-century Islamic traveler, Muhammad ibn Jubayr, born in Andalusia, and who travelled via Sicily and the Crusader states as far as Mecca. Memmi may have read his *Voyages*, translated into French by Maurice Gaudefroy-Demonbynes (Paris: Geuthner, 1949), or an even earlier French translation published in 1846. Ibn Jubayr's description of a sea battle and siege involving Saladin may have been the inspiration for one of Memmi's chapters on the battles of al-Kahin. See Paul M. Cobb, *The Race for Paradise: An Islamic History of the Crusades* (Oxford: Oxford Univ. Press, 2014), 195.

13. Walter J. Fischel, *Ibn Khaldûn and Tamerlane: Their Historic Meeting in Damascus, 1401 A.D.* (Berkeley and Los Angeles: Univ. of California Press, 1952); *Ibn Khaldûn in Egypt* (Berkeley and Los Angeles: Univ. of California Press, 1967).

More importantly, the fascinating biography of Ibn Khaldun—indeed, material for a historical novel—foreshadows several events and attitudes in *The Desert.* They include Ibn Khaldun's diplomatic mission to Pedro the Cruel in Spain, his fear for his life in Tamerlane's presence, and his desire to flatter the conqueror while impressing him with his own knowledge and wisdom. The figure of Ibn Khaldun is particularly appropriate in Memmi's novel for several reasons: his dual roles as actor in and chronicler of history, the tension between the active and the contemplative life, his unique imagining of a logic to history while living in the midst of turmoil, the diplomatic cunning he is forced to employ merely to survive, and lastly, that he was Muslim rather than Jewish, which allows *The Desert* to reflect the close historical experience of people of the two religions in North Africa. Thus the historical material—that is, Ibn Khaldun's biography and the facts he and others provide—is the catalyst for Memmi's imaginative constructions. These have a superficial resemblance to facts but a purpose which is basically novelistic, the celebration in literature of the cultural past.

The aesthetic perception of history in *The Desert* suggests models of wisdom and virtuous living and revives traditional North African forms. The impulse to bring this literary and cultural tradition to life and recall a kind of wisdom both ancient and modern is not mere nostalgia, but a serious attempt to embody a philosophy of cyclical return in history. At the same time, a tension is set up between individual and community, as the alternating guardians and conveyors of wisdom.

Thus references to the existence of the destroyed historical kingdom are less important to *The Desert* than the lives of scholars and viziers, whose experiences in North African medieval courts often resembled those of al-Mammi. Despite its echoes of history, the kingdom's very name—Le Royaume du Dedans, Kingdom of Within—suggests its insubstantiality. Rather than being about the pursuit of political power, the action of the novel is a search for the Kingdom of Within. Its movement is away from a physical kingdom and toward an inner kingdom of *sagesse*, of wisdom. The almost explicit transformation of al-Mammi's ambition parallels the redirecting of the political ambitions of defeated peoples into a striving for moral and spiritual perfectibility. Memmi commented on this in our interview with wry humor:

> Devant l'effondrement administrative, El-Mammi découvre que la seule vraie conquête, c'est la conquête de soi . . . Ce qui compte c'est de rentrer en soi-même, la voie interne, la sagesse. La sagesse, c'est toujours faute de mieux. . . .
>
> (In the face of administrative collapse, al-Mammi discovers that the only real conquest is the conquest of self . . . What counts is to go into one's self, the internal way, wisdom. Wisdom, it's always for lack of something better . . .)

In this sense, *The Desert* has the quality of a bildungsroman, with character being formed through a renunciation and a process of individuation. It is worth discussing the specific nature of al-Mammi's growth. Through his pursuit of wisdom, the imaginative recreation of the North African past in *The Desert* avoids the earlier abstractness of *La Statue de sel (Pillar of Salt)* and *Agar (Strangers)*, allowing the authentic values of North African culture to emerge through its various forms of wisdom. These original values are modified, one must remember, by being seen also from a Western and twentieth-century viewpoint.

North African values can be seen underlying the kinds of wisdom shown in *The Desert*, which can be analyzed from three directions: first, by looking at the form wisdom takes; second, at the ideal of wisdom being suggested; and third, at the community or group to which the wisdom applies. Four different kinds of wisdom occur to a greater or lesser extent in the novel and stand out in the light of these approaches. Some critical attention has been given to the scope of community and the individual's relation to it in Memmi's early novels. Isaac Yetiv proposed and applied a scheme in which concentric circles express the protagonist's expanding awareness of linkages to a community.[14] The scope of the communities involved in *The Desert* is not as concentric (focusing on the protagonist) as it was before, befitting a far from autobiographical novel. Because Memmi pays more attention to some aspects of it than to others, the scheme is, of course, fragmentary. It should indicate, though, how literary genre and technique express the relations between individual and community through ideals of wisdom.

The formal element of the epic conveys the first kind of wisdom, a nomadic ideal. This nomadic wisdom corresponds to the broad community of Berberie, comprising the indigenous Berber tribes that ruled North Africa before the Arab invasion. Saying that he wished *The Desert* to reflect "mes appartenances diverses" (my various cultural identifications)[15] Memmi emphasized that "je voulais en même temps faire un roman de la Berberie soumise, conquise, reconquise . . ." (I wanted at the same time to create a novel about the submission, conquest, reconquest, of Berberie . . .) The centuries of shared history thus mean that North Africans of Berber stock, whether Muslims or Jews, have far more in common than in contrast.

Despite having verbally espoused the idea of a Berberie that antedates religious differences, Memmi has used it only sporadically as an imaginative and formal element. Thus the wisdom of Berberie consists of the hard, primitive maxims of nomadic ancestors, received in

14. Isaac Yetiv, in *Le Thème de l'aliénation dans le roman maghrébin d'expression française 1952-1956* (Sherbrooke: CELEF, 1972), 145–201 provide a basic introduction to Memmi's early novels and placeh them in relation to those of other North African novelists.

15. A statement in another interview also indicates Memmi's belief in an ideal cultural synthesis in North Africa: "il me fallait un héros representative du Maghreb . . . si j'avais pris un prince juif ou chrétien, il aurait risqué d'être trop typé. Notez bien que mon héros n'est pas non plus tellement musulman." (I needed a hero who would be representative of the Maghreb . . . if I had created a Jewish or Christian prince, he would have risked being too stereotyped. Notice also that my hero is not so Muslim either.) Jean-Louis de Rambures, "Albert Memmi, conteur arabe," *Le Monde*, December 16, 1977, 17, 19.

a disjointed state and accepted on faith rather than understood. The founding ancestor of the tribe is reported to have declared:

"Notre peuple . . . est le plus vieux de la terre; seuls doivent compter pour nous le sang et la filiation . . . Qui a vécu dans la soie ne peut plus monter à cheval" (182–83). (Our people, he affirmed, is the oldest one on earth; only blood and blood ties must count for us . . . whoever has lived in silk can no longer ride a horse) (146).

Aphorisms like these quoted would obviously fall within the type of proverbial wisdom. In addition, this nomadic mode of wisdom relates to the genre of romance or heroic epic, "l'histoire de geste, la grande geste, des juifs du Maghreb," (the history of heroic deeds, of chivalry, of the Jews of the Maghreb), which Memmi suggested as being one of his aims. It would perhaps share the characteristics of North African epic poems, such as an anonymous work from about the fourteenth century, the Romance of Antar. Memmi's tales of wars, brigands, and battles seem to take up the Antar theme.

One element, romantic love, is absent from Memmi's novel, except for al-Mammi's temporary infatuation with the daughter of the king of Castile. The "moral" of this tale is that romance must not be allowed under any circumstances to interfere with affairs of state. A traditional ethic might be expected to provide in some way for preservation of the line, but one of the few direct references to al-Mammi's relations with women is advice both ascetic and amoral: "Use ou abuse des femmes, selon ton tempérament . . . mais après l'amour, regagne ta couche, car il faut dormer seul." (Use or abuse women, as your temperament dictates . . . But after love, then return to your couch, for you should sleep alone) (79).

Relations between the sexes are almost peripheral to the development of al-Mammi's personal ethic. Except for al-Mammi's occasional expression of a desire for sons, traditional wisdom relating to marriage and children is virtually omitted. The treatment of Castile and the romantic episode with Dolores is highly ironic, almost farcical. Memmi's novel (though its title is of cinema epic proportions) thus alludes to historical and romantic epic while carefully distancing itself from the genre through irony. The nomadic epic is represented only by certain touches of atmosphere and fragmented maxims, while the form of the oral epic is also absent. Memmi creates the impression of a once vigorous culture, which now can only be evoked in fragments of its forms and wisdom.

The second type of wisdom that the novel recalls is a religious ideal, the wisdom toward which the mystic aspires. The Sufi orders and practices in North Africa, and the traditional reverence for saints and mystics of both religions by followers of each, constitute the traditional scope of the community. The interesting figure of al-Mammi's mentor, Younous, apparently alludes to this transcendental wisdom. Historically a Sufi teacher of seventeenth-century Syria, Younous is portrayed in Sufi tales as attempting to transcend scientific knowledge for spiritual knowledge.[16] The Younous of *The Desert* does not tell stories himself, but rather gives practical, if sometimes cynical, advice of the sort quoted earlier. The moral drawn at the close of each anecdote, and the general philosophical conclusion of *The Desert*, link it to the form of Sufi tales. But their main elements, allegory and spiritual symbolism, are present only to a small extent. Although he seems attracted by the inner life, al-Mammi acquires a skeptical, stoical philosophy, the essence of his worldly experiences rather than the result of illumination from above. His frequent irony, directed at himself or others, is the expression of a man whose life has been spent in courts where appearance is all, one whose actions have been frustrated, and who begins to suspect that perhaps there is nothing to history beyond surface spectacle:

> Comme au spectacle, on peu toujours se demander à qui le tour maintenant de croire triompher? A qui le tour de commencer à mourir? Car le seul triomphe définitif est celui de la mort. (188)

16. Yunus, son of Adam, died in 1670. Idries Shah attributes to him the tale "The Food of Paradise" in *Tales of the Dervishes* (New York: Dutton, 1970; rpt. 1993), 15–20.

> (As at a spectacle, one can always ask whose turn it is to think he is triumphing, and whose turn it is to begin dying. For death alone triumphs in the end). (151)

Memmi thus alludes to North African traditions of transcendent, religious wisdom, but, since his irony constantly undermines it, does not genuinely appropriate this form of wisdom in *The Desert.*

Al-Mammi's third kind of wisdom, a skeptical and ironic type, is produced by situations in which a man of contemplative nature must look first of all to his political survival. In this medieval community of despots, courtiers, and scholars, al-Mammi finds friends and employment through his skills of eloquence and penmanship. The parts of the novel relating incidents in the courts of Fez and Tunis, and Tamerlane's court, are the most vivid and fascinating of all. Al-Mammi must employ all his gifts in the genre of "advice to princes," both those of a storyteller who delights in embroidering on his experiences, and those of a diplomat. Each of these talents requires that the speaker first of all please his audience.

The Desert has connections, both geographical and formal, with Oriental stories. They include written tales, such as the *Arabian Nights*, and oral tales, such as the North African *khurafa* stories.[17]

17. Memmi ascribes his technique to Jewish and Arab influences, including *khurafa*, which he absorbed as a child: "Cette manière de raconter est une manière que j'ai sucée avec le lait de ma mère . . . Ma mère m'a raconté des centaines d'histoires. L'une des sources de ces contes était le magasin de mon père. Chaque fois que mon père s'en allait faire des commissions, l'ouvrier me racontait des histoires . . . C'est une habitude, ce n'est pas que j'ai choisi cette method de travailler en quittant la tradition occidentale . . . Par exemple, une histoire dans une histoire, ça j'entendue des milliers de fois." (This way of telling stories is something I absorbed with my mother's milk. One source for these tales was my father's workshop. Whenever my father went off to do some errands, the worker would tell me stories. . . . It's a habit, it's not that I chose this way of working by leaving the Western tradition . . . For example, a tale within a tale, I've heard that thousands of times.) He mentions a didactic use: "l'habitude, au lieu de donner une explication, de raconter une histoire à la place: 'Tu vas comprendre mieux, je vais te raconter une histoire . . . '" (the habit,

Memmi's novel recalls an Arabic written form, *maqāmāt*, short topics linked by a narrator or traveler,[18] and is also reminiscent of Islamic travel accounts. The semifictional frame of the narration and succession of storytellers are typical of Oriental tales in general, and deserve to be examined in detail.

The frame of the novel is entitled "Ce qu'en disent les historiens" (What Historians Have to Say). This passage is a first-person introduction giving the purported historical setting of al-Mammi's narrative and concluding, "Voici le récit que fit mon ancêtre, Jubaïr Ouali El-Mammi, à Timur Lang, dit le Conquérant Boiteux" (13). (Here is the tale that my ancestor, Jubair Wali al-Mammi, told Timur Lang, called the Lame Conqueror) (2). The author has thus adopted the mask of a fictional narrator called Albert Memmi reporting "What the Historians Have to Say," and giving the reader imaginary historical data suiting the narrative requirements of the novel. The novelist's imagination is discreetly veiled behind a public voice, presented as common knowledge or tradition handed down through the generations. "Mon ancêtre était alors, dit-on, un beau vieillard presque sexagénaire . . ." (12). (My ancestor was by then a handsome old man almost in his sixties, they say) (2). With the appearance of "*dit-on*" (they say) the transition is completed into the realm of the imagination. From then on, the second fictional narrator, al-Mammi himself, comes to occupy the center of the stage, even in the "author's introduction." His listeners immediately begin to admire his discretion and diplomacy when, suddenly the center of attention in Tamerlane's court, he modestly declines to advise the monarch, then yields in a presumed compliment to his questioner's intelligence:

---

instead of giving an explanation, of telling a story instead: "You'll understand better if I tell you this story . . .")

18. For examples of *maqāmāt*, see Ilse Lichtenstadter, *Introduction to Classical Arabic Literature: With Selections from Representative Works in English Translation* (New York: Schocken, 1976), 112–14, 340–41; see also James Kritzeck, ed., *Anthology of Islamic Literature from the Rise of Islam to Modern Times* (1964; New York: Meridian, 1975), 224–36.

> El-Mammi d'abord se déroba: "Seigneur, on ne conseille pas un roi . . ." Puis, sur l'insistance de son interlocuteur, demanda la permission de raconter sa propre vie et ses aventures à travers le monde. Le Conquérant y trouverait peut-être sa réponse. (12–13)
>
> (Al-Mammi was evasive at first: "Sire, one does not counsel a king." Then, as his questioner insisted, he asked permission to retell his own life and adventures across the world. Perhaps the Conqueror would find his answer in al-Mammi's own story.) (2)

The first chapter opens then with the words, "Si je suis né dans la capital, je n'y ai guère demeuré" (17). (Though I was born in the capital, I have scarcely lived there) (3). The rest of the novel, until the final pages, continues in the voice of this second fictional narrator, al-Mammi, recounting his adventures and peregrinations which culminate in his present captivity and audience.

His listeners in Damascus must find the stranger's stories unusually entertaining as he ranges over diverse aspects of Maghrebian life. It is another matter whether they would believe all that they hear. Some may have been aware that al-Kahin was connected to the story of a famous queen, Kahena, who like al-Kahin alienated her allies by ravaging the countryside and was betrayed by her sons.[19] His listeners may or may not believe the stories of naked savages beyond the desert who made al-Mammi their ruler. Al-Mammi is probably the most convincing when describing situations closest to his home, which is

19. Dahya or Dihya La Kahena is an important semi-historical, semi-mythological figure in North African Jewish consciousness. Perhaps the ruler of Judeo-Berber tribes, she is said to had been the leader of the indigenous resistance against the Arab Muslim invasions of the late seventh century. Ibn Khaldun recounts her story. Betrayed by her own sons to the enemy, she was killed by a well, a lake, or on the seashore. She has been revered as a heroine by both Muslims and Jews and has been a potent resistance symbol and rallying cry in modern times. In the 1920s the Jewish intellectuals of the "Alliance School" of Tunis founded a publishing house, Editions La Kahéna. See, for example, Didier Nebot, *La Kahéna: Reine d'Ifrikia* (Paris: Editions Carrière, 1998).

already exotic enough for his audience: the pleasant life in the court of Tunis, contrasted with Machiavellian power games in Fez, and life among brigands in the North African mountains.

Al-Mammi seems to have seized the occasion of recounting his adventures to adopt some of the traditional modes of storytellers. In politeness to his guest, Tamerlane evidently pretends to believe everything he hears, while perhaps enjoying the stories for themselves. The superficial genre is that of advice to princes, but much of the speaker's craft lies in enthralling his audience. At the close of the novel, Memmi the narrator again addresses his readers directly:

> Vous aimeriez savoir si Tamerlan a suivi les conseils de mon ancêtre? La réponse est non. Le grand conquérant fit de Balkh sa capital. Au reste, cela est bien connue: et assurément, vous ne me posez ces questions que par modéstie . . . Car Balkh a été prise et rasée à son tour. (190)
>
> (Would you like to know whether Tamerlane followed my ancestor's advice? The answer is that he didn't. The great conqueror made Balkh his capital. As for the rest, it's well known; and I'm sure that you're only asking me these questions out of modesty . . . For Balkh was taken and razed to the ground when its turn came). (152–53)

Thus even on the semi-fictional level in which the first narrator speaks, the *conteur* (storyteller) with his delight in suspense and gentle flattery of his audience has ousted the *chroniqueur* (chronicler).

The frame situation itself recalls familiar literary settings. Al-Mammi, the exiled prince of an enemy people, is suspect to Tamerlane, and his life hangs on the whim of the conqueror. A few poorly chosen words would have quickly condemned him: like Scheherezade's, his life depends upon capturing his listener's imagination. Memmi himself mentioned the influence of the *Arabian Nights* on his novel. Apart from al-Mammi's dangerous situation, which frames the stories, the Chinese box arrangement of tales within tales and the prodigious and unrestrained inventiveness of the traditional stories are present only intermittently, through allusion. Al-Mammi's situation differs concretely from Scheherezade's since he seems under compulsion to compress rather than extend his narrative. This compression leads to a terseness and economy that the contemporary reader can appreciate. Another difference between *The Desert* and the *Arabian Nights* lies in the purposefulness of Memmi's anecdotes. His narrative's basic impulse is presenting a world view and a model for personal ethics.[20]

The fourth kind of wisdom, a moralizing impulse, links *The Desert* more closely to another oral genre which Memmi mentioned, the *khurafa* or traditional stories still told in Tunisia (see note 18).They are purely oral tales, never written nor collected until modern times. Anthropologists claim that the stories express most closely the collective, popular Tunisian mind, and they have always fascinated children. Two types exist, corresponding to the deepest division in Tunisian life: tales told by men and those told by women:

> Les contes d'hommes viriles ou respectables comportent toujours une morale et une bonne morale. Quant aux femmes . . . disons que leurs contes se moquent éperdûment de la morale, du conformisme et peuvent à l'occasion être fort grivois.
>
> (The stories by virile and respectable men always include a moral, a good moral. As for women . . . let's say that their stories make endless fun of morality and conformism, and can sometimes be quite off-color).[21]

20. The *Arabian Nights* have been described as primarily "ornamental, variations on the world, not completions of it; neither are they lessons, structures, extensions, or totalities designed to illustrate either the author's prowess in representation, the education of a character, or ways in which the world can be viewed and changed." Edward W. Said, *Beginnings: Intention and Method* (New York: Basic Books, 1975; rpt. New York: Columbia Univ. Press, 1985), 81. *The Desert*, in contrast, partakes of most of the tendencies mentioned, especially the last two.

21. Abdelwahab Bouhdiba, *L'Imaginaire maghrébin: Etudes de dix contes pour enfants* (Tunis: Maison tunisienne del'Edition, 1977), 17.

Of the rich veins of women's tales and men's, it appears that those of the latter group have had the more obvious repercussions in *The Desert.* Generally, the women's tales deal with flesh-eating ogres, and other fantastic themes, easily psychoanalyzed into sexual symbolism. The men's *khurafa*, in contrast, draw morals to be applied in community and public life or consist of worldly and practical wisdom. Younous often echoes them: self-sufficiency, loyalty to one's employer, and the maximum use of one's powers of practical intellect are some of the lessons of survival which al-Mammi gradually learns. In this sense his anecdotes echo the Tunisian men's *khurafa.*

One of the names in the novel, though not the character which bears it, is reminiscent of a stock figure in the women's *khurafa.* It is the brigand al-Ghoul, in the traditional tales an ogre who seduces and marries young maidens only to dine off them later. In the novel, however, he is a primitive, simple-hearted brigand with whom al-Mammi for a while throws in his lot. Besides content, Memmi's incidents differ in form from the oral tales. They lack the repeated adages and rhymes that seem to be the focal points of *khurafa.*[22] Overall, though, Memmi has kept the moralizing impulse of Tunisian man's *khurafa.*

The tales of Joha, or Nasrudin, are also probably evoked in *The Desert.* Al-Mammi shares a few of this ambiguous character's traits: he is somewhat crafty, wise in a practical way, socially marginal, and more often than he likes ends up looking ridiculous. Though al-Mammi always maintains the highest moral principles, he sometimes finds his calculations are turned against him, and becomes ridiculous in his own eyes. The humor in the novel is subtle and introspective, never slapstick, and al-Mammi's royal origins make him far different from Joha, who is often a small shopkeeper or an illiterate peasant.[23]

22. For example, Bouhdiba, 17–18.

23. Jean Déjeux, *Djoh'a, Héros de la tradition orale arabo-berbère hier et aujourd'hui* (Sherbrook: Naaman, 1978), 21, writes that this discussion of Joha's characteristics (21–26) is inspired by a lecture of Memmi's entitled "La Personnalité de Jeha dans la literature orale des Arabes et des Juifs." Memmi also mentioned in

The Desert echoes the more didactic purposes of the Arabic, and specifically Tunisian, anecdotal literature. The novel's values of skeptical wisdom, self-control, and political acumen reflect the civilization of North African medieval courts. Memmi has also remembered the first duty of the storyteller: to amaze and amuse.

Subtle humor tints many of the characters in *The Desert*: the narrator describes their excesses, indulgences, and quirks with sympathetic irony. It extends to kings and their counselors of almost all nations (the obese and pleasure-loving king of Tunis, the exotic Castilians, and the Burntfaces) but this irony is directed above all at al-Mammi the protagonist, by al-Mammi the narrator. On his ambassadorial visit to Castile, the protagonist ridicules the Castilian customs, until he falls under the spell of Dolores, when they suddenly appear comprehensible and dignified. The way in which each civilization signifies status is ridiculed. The Burntfaces denote prestige among themselves by the height of their feathers; the North Africans by the height of their turbans; and the Spanish by the height of their heels, says al-Mammi. His cosmopolitan experiences thus give him a relativistic view which he expresses in humorous irony toward many cultures, including his own. It is difficult to say whether this irony is designed merely to entertain Tamerlane (it never extends to the Mongols) or is a superimposed trait, the attitude of the modern narrator.

The humor based on relativism in *The Desert* raises the question of whether or not its Maghrebian aspects are challenged and possibly overshadowed by a prevailing Western and European viewpoint. The practical wisdom is also evident in European picaresque novels; the art of the courtier and the art of governing are fully expressed in European genres. Some of al-Mammi's fundamental attitudes, giving rise to his irony, also exist in a French current of literary introspection. His mixing a life of action with one of contemplation

---

the interview that the traditional stories of Joha partially inspired *The Desert*. See also Guy Dugas, *La Littérature judéo-maghrébine d'expression française: Entre Djéha et Cagayous* (Paris: L'Harmattan, 1990).

resembles an Existentialist choice; al-Mammi's desert recalls that of Saint-Exupéry.[24]

Memmi's novel is close in philosophy and form to another European work, Montaigne's *Essais* (*Essays*) (1580). Memmi declines anything other than a private motive in publishing his book, as did Montaigne in his preface:

> C'est icy un livre de bonne foy, lecteur. Il t'advertit dès l'entrée, que je ne m'y suis propose aucune fin, que domestique et privée. Je veus qu'on m'y voie en ma façon simple, naturelle et ordinaire, sans contentions et artifice: car c'est moy que je peins . . . Ainsi, lecteur, je suis moy-mesmes la matière de mon livre . . . [25]
>
> (Reader, loe here a well-meaning Booke. It doth at the first entrance forewarne thee, that in contriving the same I have proposed unto my selfe no other than a familiar and private end: I desire therein to be delineated in mine own genuine, simple and ordinarie fashion, without contention, art or study; for it is myselfe I pourtray).

Al-Mammi's report of his visit to the Burntfaces resembles Montaigne's "Des Cannibales" (On Cannibals)[26] in both cultural relativity and use of savages to expose the vanities of one's own civilization. Memmi's hero's stoic and skeptical conclusions resemble Montaigne's meditations on death in "Que philosopher, c'est apprendre à mourir" (To Philosophize is to Learn to Die).[27]

Another readily available influence for Memmi has likely been Montesquieu's *Lettres persanes* (The Persian Letters) (1721). The tales

24. For example, p. 20 "Je conquis patiemmement le désert, et surtout je m'apprivoisai moi-même." (I was patiently conquering the desert, and above all I was taming myself.) (7).

25. *Les Essais de Michel de Montaigne*, ed. Pierre Villey (Paris: Presses universitaires, 1965), "Au lecteur." Preface to Montaigne's *Essays*, trans. John Florio, ed. Ben Schneider (Portland: Renascence Editions), pages.uoregon.edu/rbear/Montaigne/#p1. Trans. pub. 1603, 1904, rpt. 1910, 1921.

26. Montaigne, *Essais*, 202–14.

27. Montaigne, *Essais*, 81–96.

of Uzbek the Persian king and his minister Rica, their adventures, and reactions on visiting the exotic countries of Europe, particularly France, with its inscrutable customs, have influenced many European satirical and ironical writers, and no doubt Memmi, too. Uzbek's tales of a primitive people, the Troglodytes, who pass from selfishness to altruism, resemble al-Mammi's descriptions of exotic peoples such as the Burntfaces, while his portrayals of French customs resemble al-Mammi's reactions to the Castilians.[28]

It becomes almost impossible to assign comparative strength to the various currents, Western and Eastern, secular and religious, to which *The Desert* alludes. The European novel itself owes its origins to Oriental genres. European secular Renaissance philosophy was inspired by a classical tradition which had been preserved in medieval Islamic learning. In *The Desert* the historical reality of a Maghrebian Judeo-Islamic tradition is evident even when its author appears to translate some of its terms into Western philosophical references.

The novel's view of history, as al-Mammi expresses it to Tamerlane, appears to be cyclical. The state (people, or tribe, in al-Mammi's terminology) is an organic being engaged in a process of individuation, and destined like all organisms for decline and death: "la vie d'un peuple n'est qu'une longue conquête de soi-même; lorqu'elle touche à son terme, il n'a plus qu'à mourir" (184–85). (The life of a people is only a long conquest of itself; when it reaches its end, all it has to do is die) (148).

These meditations seem to express a Romantic, Hegelian view that history is the unfolding of national spirit, combined with Spengler's emphasis on inevitable decline. But the theories of Ibn Khaldun, the model for El-Mammi's life, provide an even closer resemblance. Ibn

28. For an English translation, see Montesquieu, *The Persian Letters* trans. and intro. George Healey (Indianapolis/Cambridge: Hackett Publishing, 1964; rpt. 1999). A French edition that Memmi might have used is Charles de Secondat, Baron de Montesquieu, *Les Lettres persanes* (Paris: Livres de poche, 1968).

Khaldun's *Muqaddimah* (Introduction to History) (1381) develops a similar view of dynasties and their decline into "senility":

> The life span of a dynasty corresponds to the life span of an individual; it grows up and passes into an age of stagnation and thence into retrogression.[29]

During its life's course, a dynasty passes from desert savagery and bravery, with strong group solidarity, to a sedentarized civilization of luxury and plenty, and finally decadence, senility, and the decline of solidarity. At its end the civilization possesses only the emblems of power and lacks any will for self-defense.[30] Ibn Khaldun's analysis finds echo in al-Mammi's description of the decadence and defeat of his own kingdom:

> Notre people rougissait lorsqu'on lui parlait de tentes et de nomades. C'étaient des temps bien révolus; depuis si longtemps il y avait de l'eau en abundance et de l'ombre, qu'il ne voulait plus se souvenir que l'ombre fut celle des lances et l'eau gagnée par les grands chameliers. (184)

> (Our people blushed when tents and nomads were mentioned. Times had really changed: there had been water in abundance and shade for so long, that our people no longer wanted to remember that the shade was the shade of lances and the water was won by the great camel drivers). (147)

Memmi has attempted to convey imaginatively Ibn Khaldun's theoretical analysis of the rise and fall of civilizations. *The Desert* shows the savagery and energy of nomadic life, the peak of civilization, and

29. Ibn Khaldun, trans. Franz Rosenthal, ed. N. J. Dawood, *The Muqaddimah: An Introduction to History* (Princeton, NJ: Princeton Univ. Press, 1967, 2005), 138. The editor states, "To Ibn Khaldûn, 'dynasty' and 'state' signify one and the same thing—the word he uses is 'dawlah'" (xli).

30. Ibn Khaldun, *Muqaddimah*, 137.

its final decline. The state thus easily fell before the greater energies of the Great Nomad, Tamerlane. "Votre avant-garde touchait les premières tours de guet, que le Conseil discutait encore de l'impôt sur le sel" (184). (Your advance guard was reaching the first watch towers, while the Council was still arguing about the salt tax) (148).

Both Memmi's and Ibn Khaldun's work convey a sense of inevitability in the destruction of civilizations. It leads in the novel to an evocation of the "Ubi sunt?" theme, a lament for the passing of grandeur and nobility. Though the massacre of his people and the obliteration of his kingdom have an appearance of finality, Memmi the narrator hints at a possible rebirth through the person of al-Mammi, "souverain-fondateur d'une dynastie nouvelle" (190).(founding sovereign of a new dynasty) (153). The "Ubi sunt?" mood is more than mere nostalgia. Some achievement, some grains of wisdom perhaps, survive the destruction and form the basis of a new civilization.

This cyclical idea is also embodied in the shape of the novel. It may be seen in the narrative movement from exile to return and then to exile again. It emerges in the development of the various types of wisdom, in al-Mammi's progression from not knowing what to desire, to his attaining wisdom and thence to not desiring anything. The cyclical idea affects the form of *The Desert* in its series of frames, each enclosing the other. The novelist's illusion is created step by step. The words of the contemporary narrator in the introduction frame al-Mammi's words to Tamerlane, which in turn frame the narration. At the end, the novel returns to the two original narrators.[31] The gradual increase in fictional intensity and gradual withdrawal from the illusion create the impression that fiction is only one of several alternative ways to truth, that this novelist does not claim that fiction has a unique authority.

31. John McCormick, *Fiction as Knowledge: The Modern Post-Romantic Novel* (1975; New Brunswick, NJ: Transaction Press, 1999), 6, would apply to *The Desert*: "The cyclical idea enhances the illusion through which the novelist's kind of knowledge can be conveyed."

Thus we need to remember the other pens in Memmi's quiver: the pens of the sociologist, political writer, philosopher, and public intellectual and, as we have been reminded recently, theoretician.[32]

Thus the complex, well-balanced, and careful construction of *The Desert* brings into Western focus the cultural dilemmas of Maghrebian life and fiction. From the point of view of the novelist's art, because of its limited and precise aim, it is even more successful than Memmi's earlier novels. The framework is not as purely North African or Middle Eastern as it might appear on first sight, but the subject matter combines some genuinely indigenous concerns of Memmi's original culture with philosophical elements shared by East and West. His techniques owe much to North African oral folktales. The form of wisdom thus stressed is a largely personal interpretation of his ancestors' wisdom, but is integrated successfully into the novel. Memmi is concerned with both literary experiment and preservation of his tradition, transposed into the novel. Paradoxically, this fact also places *The Desert* within the tradition of historical vision and cyclical return of the modern post-Romantic novel. A largely Western ironic tone distances the narrators from the protagonist and his world, however, and dilutes this Romantic impulse. While the novel draws on many sources both Western and Eastern, *The Desert*'s basic impulse to breathe new life into the forms and history of Maghrebian Arab-Jewish identity is Memmi's most original contribution to the genre as yet.

The Desert is a careful effort to integrate the traditions, concerns, and literary structures closest to the novelist. The novel has still not completely left the pale of autobiography, but Memmi's historical perspective gives greater substance and aesthetic significance to autobiography than it had before. The reader should agree that Memmi has

32. See the groundbreaking recent study by Lia Nicole Brozgal, *Against Autobiography: Albert Memmi and the Production of Theory* (Lincoln: Univ. of Nebraska Press, 2013). Against the current of most Memmi criticism, Brozgal situates Memmi as an influential theorist.

been fully successful in his professed aim of entertaining both himself and his audience. The author's own words, revealing the modesty and care of a craftsman, serve as an introduction to *The Desert*: "Je me suis beaucoup amusé à le faire, et j'espère que cela fera autant de plaisir à le lire." (I got a lot of enjoyment out of writing it, and I hope readers will have just as much pleasure in reading it.)

The Desert

What Historians Have to Say

I promised—some years ago now—to bring out the chronicle of the Kingdom of Within fairly quickly. Life has not let me.

My few readers, those who still have faith in me, deserve not to be kept in suspense, so I have decided to bring out separately this portion devoted to the life and adventures of Jubair Wali al-Mammi. My readers may recall that this is my oldest known ancestor, with the exception, of course, of the Numidian prince who appears on horseback on Mr. Rousset's Punic medal, the one I reproduced in The Scorpion.

You can see that The Desert *is in the same vein as my previous novels. The subject is still the history of our family, or tribe, or whatever you like to call it. As always, I have tried to be as truthful as possible, and respectful of tradition.*

Anyway, here is what historians have to say:

In the Gurara, in the extreme north of the Touat region between Tamentit and Sba-Gerara, there existed a small independent kingdom, the Kingdom of Within, which survived until the fifteenth century. We know about its language, customs, and institutions; we even have details about the disaster that brought about its end.

The credit for passing down this knowledge is mainly due to my ancestor, Jubair Wali al-Mammi, who did his best to write the chronicle of his native land, under circumstances that he himself describes.

It was in 1392, after a decisive assault by Tamerlane, followed by an almost total massacre of the population, that the Kingdom of Within ceased to exist. Eight years later, in 1400 to be exact, in the city of

Damascus, which had been sacked in turn by the same conqueror, al-Mammi was paying obeisance to the victor.

My ancestor was by then a handsome old man almost in his sixties, they say; he was wearing "a turban of raw silk and a burnoose as finely-woven as his wit, in its color resembling the first shades of night." This garment attracted the attention of the great Conqueror, who said, "That man there is not one of ours." Al-Mammi thereupon introduced himself.

Tamerlane, his interest aroused by his captive, invited him to his table and asked him to explain why the collapse of the Kingdom of Within had been so rapid. Since Tamerlane had just then conquered the illustrious city of Balkh, and was considering making it his capital, he asked for Jubair's advice: what should he do to prevent this city, of which he had such high hopes, from succumbing to the same ill fate?

Al-Mammi was evasive at first: "Sire, one does not counsel a king." Then, as his questioner insisted, he asked permission to retell his own life and adventures across the world. Perhaps the Conqueror would find his answer in al-Mammi's own story.

Here is the tale that my ancestor, Jubair Wali al-Mammi, told Timur Lang, called the Lame Conqueror.

Younous

Though I was born in the capital, I have scarcely lived there. Because of the misfortune that fell on our family, I have spent most of my life in the provinces and exposed to the vagaries of foreign courts. Even when my cousin the king let me come back, it was only to witness the death agonies of my unhappy land, as if the fates had decided once and for all that I should remain the eternal outsider.

This is not to deny the fact that I have found in exile both honor and profit. The day following my return, I paid the king a visit. Since there was no seat for me close enough to him, I squatted down on my heels. The monarch gave me a stern, amazed stare, then suddenly burst out laughing. I was familiar with this laugh of his: it welled up from our shared childhood, before the laugh had become set in that royal frown. Touched, he fired at me:

"You Bedouin, you!"

I also sensed a certain disdain in his tone. If only he knew how much I felt I owed to my spell of exile, despite all the misery and loneliness! The wandering life, from Tunis to Tlemcen, from Fez to Castile, from Cairo to Damascus, by not letting me form attachments to anything or anyone, has kept me for myself, which is really the only true freedom.

I will pass over in silence that first part of my life, spent in the old palace, which was at the bottom of the Royal Park and backed against the wall of the old cemetery. Nor will I describe the circumstances of my father's death and the usurpation of the throne. Nothing can be known for sure about these events. Am I really my father's

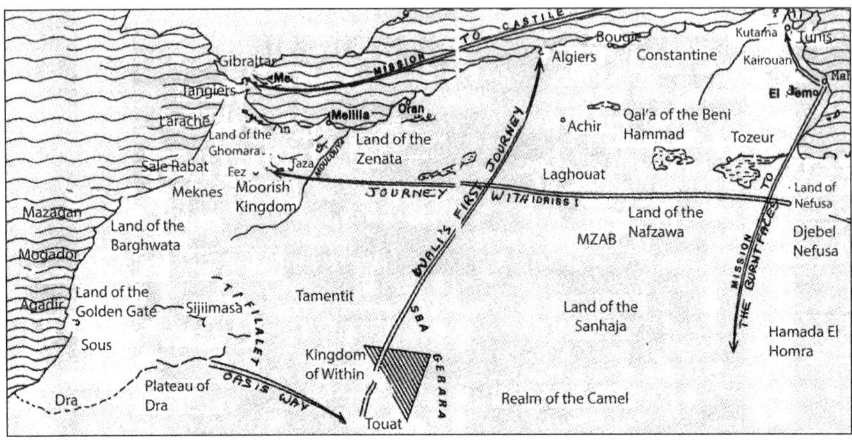

1. "In the Gurara, there existed a small independent kingdom." Courtesy of Albert Memmi.

son, as my mother has always affirmed? Or perhaps I am a belated and illegitimate fruit, with no right to the throne at all, as my uncle and his son, each in turn the recognized sovereign of the kingdom, have held? My mother and uncle have both now been dead for some while. No one can ever be sure of the circumstances of his birth; a man's childhood is hardly his own; who can ever claim that he has shaped his own destiny?

My own destiny was launched in an extraordinary manner. That delicate colorless down, the harbinger of manhood, had hardly begun to sprout on my chin and cheeks, when the usurper dispatched me to the middle of the desert. At first I thought I was going to die. An enclosure of prickly pears through which perplexed lizards and cruel snakes slid silently; a single, doorless, low-ceilinged room with lime-washed walls; a gummy-eyed old mule resigned to the stings of the mosquitoes swarming over it; a few stupid chickens quarreling over occasional bits of grain in the mule's dung; an unruly nanny-goat scattering the yard with shiny black droppings; and finally Younous, the only slave permitted me by my royal kin. I did not know whether this servant was completely lethargic by nature or whether he had received instructions to be so. Around the enclosure, as far as the unbroken horizon, there was nothing, nothing but sand and the terrible desert light, that light of which it was impossible to guess whether it came down from the sky or radiated up out of the ground. The desert was my only bridge, albeit an impassable one, to the rest of the universe. How could I ever cross that infinity of dust and stones? Where could I turn, without exposing myself to the sun, and condemning myself to death? It was then that I learned, Sire, what it means to love the land of one's childhood! The memory of each face, each flower, affected me so much that tears came to my eyes at the idea that perhaps I would never see them again!

It was in the desert, though, that I learned this amazing truth, the foremost of all truths: it is imperative to make one's peace with oneself. It's because I discovered this truth there, that I have loved the desert with a passion; it's in order to remind myself of this truth that I have often returned to the desert. The thought of the desert has become a talisman that I have been able to invoke at will: "Remember, when you yourself had nothing and no one to depend on." Then it seems to me that nothing can touch me, at least in the kernel of my being.

One morning, I know not by what enchantment, as I woke I saw the sunshine glimmering on the ceiling of my hut as if it were reflected from the sea. I hurried outside on trembling legs: there was nothing but the usual sand and light. I discovered what was responsible for my agitation: a pan in which Younous had put a few dried peppers to soak in a little water. It made me laugh: to think that my happiness and all my surging memories could be summed up in a handful of red peppers!

Much later, when I had more confidence, I risked walking a few hundred paces without constantly looking for bearings and glancing back at my footprints. One day, when I had been distracted for a brief moment, I suddenly felt I had lost the invisible thread that, by means of a few pebbles differing almost imperceptibly from the others, a few tufts of thorn, linked me to the enclosure. I had gotten lost. I was seized by a violent desire to retrace my steps immediately; but—amid that uniformity of stone—which way was forward and which way backward? Where was north and where was south? I began running and shouting like a lost child, knowing even while I did so that it was futile . . . when, oh bliss, that big puppet's head popped up: Younous himself! I don't know whether he just happened there or whether he had followed me since the beginning of my walk; he didn't reveal anything. My fear dissolved instantly, replaced by embarrassment. I pretended not to have noticed Younous and continued shouting as if it were a game, as if I were trying to raise an echo or testing the effects of my voice in that solitude.

That moment of searing contempt for myself, experienced in front of a slave as well, did more for me than many months of effort. Why had I felt such panic? What imaginary peril had threatened me? Because I had strayed by a few yards! Even if I had been a whole league away, it would have been undignified to abandon myself thus to my body's panic. The truth was that I had been afraid of being alone.

I had learned my lesson; although I still gave in to weakness occasionally, it was because I had set myself tests that were still too hard for me. Until then, when a caravan appeared in the distance, I would jump on the mule, urging the poor beast into a trot that had long been beyond its strength. I would give the caravaneers such a festive welcome that those rough fellows, who had probably been told what kind of a prisoner I was, and that they should not come too near my enclosure, could not hide their emotion. Soon I recovered entirely the slowness and dignity proper in greeting the people of the desert. On more than one occasion, I even refrained from putting myself out for them.

"Do you prefer," I said to myself, "the company of the most ignorant and malodorous camel driver, to your own company?"

I not only undertook longer and longer walks, but even sometimes played at getting lost. I still sometimes panicked, and I was demanding too much of my strength; but one's strength should, from time to time, be pushed to its limits; it is only then that one tests oneself and one has possession of oneself. Stretching further and further the links that held me fixed to the minute enclosure in which my royal tormentor had wished to confine my existence, I was patiently conquering the desert, and above all I was taming myself. Thenceforth free of any impatience, no longer attempting to flee, I no longer felt enchained. Ultimately, when I realized that, rather than the enclosure, it was space itself in which I had felt imprisoned, then space became my own realm. The majority of men, though free according to the law, likewise during their whole lives scarcely leave little shops or rooms hardly wider than tombs: it is because they would feel ill if they had to be alone.

It was as if I were waking from a mirage that had troubled my eyes and sapped my spirit. I explained to Younous that I no longer wanted to be entirely dependent on him, and I put myself to work: milking the goat, exercising the mule, and caring for the chickens. The days slipped past, framed as always by the morning and evening prayers, but this frame now had something to fill it.

I also discovered how rich, varied, and populous the desert is, and how no unjust threat exists, for no animal in it, except for man sometimes, attacks without reason. Even the snake does not attack unless its body is stepped on, and the scorpion unless it believes itself in danger. One night I awoke with the unpleasant sensation that there was a creature crawling on my bare arm; in the moonlight, I saw a tawny scorpion. If I had moved, if I had panicked, I would have been stung to death. The small creature hesitated, went forward an inch, and then ran off over the bed and disappeared. The scorpion is like the hyena—it only attacks the weak. The cry of the jackal grew familiar to me and I learned to sleep more soundly, in that doorless hovel in the heart of the awesome desert, than in the middle of a palace surrounded by a thousand guards among whom one, perhaps, is an assassin.

On the nights when sleep eluded me, instead of tossing fruitlessly from side to side on my bed, I stayed until dawn crouching at the entrance to the enclosure. From the black night, I watched the slow birth of all shades and degrees of pinks, yellows, and greens, which soon fused again in the dazzling white of the day. The desert is none other than that festival of light.

A year went by, then a miracle happened: Younous started talking, and I saw that he was neither feebleminded nor dumb. The evening before, an emissary from the king had informed me that I could leave the desert and go anywhere except to the court. No doubt it was thought that I had undergone punishment enough, or that death would obviously have none of me. I expressed merely moderate satisfaction: for too long now, I had ceased to be unhappy. To be sure, I did not know whether I was happy; but if the condition, in which no desire exists without suffering, can be called happiness, then surely that was what I was. I replied that I would remain in the desert until the end of the spring.

It was then, after the messenger's departure, that Younous kissed my hand and said:

"Now you can leave, and I will come with you."

Thus he had come to consider me worthy of him, and he decided to take my side; I had won my first companion.

Younous was giving me too much credit, though; my courage was not as great as all that: I simply did not want to return to the court. Even if the king had given me the choice, it was not there that I wanted to go. I had decided first to see the world and only return to my native country with my head held high, when I could occupy my rightful position. It was too early to hope to return as anything but a man defeated. I knew I had to prove myself by living with people and this challenge, after proving myself by living with solitude, still gave me cause for fear.

So we let the spring, the most beautiful season of the desert, pass by; and then the summer, when it is not good to travel. Younous used the time well by teaching me to fight and hunt, bend the bow more skillfully, and wield the lance and sword firmly; he corrected the imperfections in my horsemanship. All this he did without becoming any more talkative than he was before the miracle. He made me a gift of a horse, a magnificent gray spotted with russet. That horse must have cost him a good deal and I wondered how he could have come by such an amount. Younous's gift gave me my first responsibility, one I fulfilled joyfully. In my enthusiasm, I spent considerable time grooming my horse, making it a point of honor to have everything about him perfect. This new task, added to the others, did not leave me time to take care of myself and often the day ended without my being absolutely presentable myself. For a long time Younous said nothing, but one evening when I had particularly neglected myself, he went and scooped up a handful of dirt and rubbed my horse's rump and chest with it, nullifying all my efforts.

"The horse must be meet for his rider," he said simply.

Another day, after watering our animals at a water hole, as we ourselves were drinking we saw a man spring up and rush toward us, shouting and shaking his lance. It was the owner of the well; we had unwittingly trespassed on his property. As fast as my trembling hands allowed me, I snatched an arrow from my quiver, put it in the bow and let fly. I was in full vigor and beginning to aim quite well, but I had shot too early: the arrow fell a good way before him. I thought we were lost: I did not have time for a second shot—I gave a shout of frustration. It was only then that Younous, who had prepared his bow without haste, aimed his weapon and let fly his arrow. We watched it sail slowly through space until it reached the horseman, who fell off his mount. The horse galloped on a little way, and silence fell again.

Still trembling, I approached the man lying there; I saw he was not yet dead. I tried to apologize for having taken his water and for having been obliged to defend ourselves. But he did not answer and did me the favor of dying, for which I was grateful to him. Younous drew the arrow from the corpse and, still without a word, handed me it. I've kept it by me ever since; it's still in my quiver, to make me always remember that getting excited is the worst course, and that one should shoot neither too early nor too late.

Younous's lessons were like that: he preferred giving them with a gesture, but they struck through to the meaning of life and the threshold of death. Just as briefly, and always with precision, he discussed with me the arts of manipulating men and seducing women, of bearing pain and facing death, of giving pleasure its due without losing oneself in it. In short, everything that as a deprived child I had not been able to learn in the court, Younous taught me.

At the beginning of autumn, Younous finally told me:

"I have nothing more to teach you, at least as long as we stay in the desert."

He was right: the time to leave had come. It was imperative, and soon. If a migratory bird does not leave at the end of the season, it will never leave. If I did not get out of the desert now, I would never get out. I had a task and I ought to remember that. I had spent enough time persuading myself I was no longer a child; now I had to find out whether I had really become a man.

The Fat King

I went first to Algiers, where I knew I would find a few of my father's former protégés who had taken refuge there after his death. They had already heard about my early sufferings and all I had to do was tell them the rest. Everyone showed pity for me, but I made the bitter discovery that pity allows us very little, in the belief that this little should suffice us in our present plight. Months passed in a futile wait for a position worthy of my birth. I was about to resign myself to accepting some humiliating occupation, when I learned that Bologuine, the all-powerful vizier of the sovereign of Tunis, was searching for a seal bearer. A fallen prince, without land or subjects, I could hope for nothing better at the moment. I therefore hastened to Tunis without sparing the horses and introduced myself at once. I was blessed with a fair hand and had earned the reputation, perhaps well so, of having a taste for study. Isolated as I was from affairs in which power might be exercised, what was there left for a wellborn young man but knowledge or the sword? Since the sword had for the moment been forbidden me, I had launched myself into books as one launches into an attack, determined to carry the day or perish. In the old pavilion at the bottom of the park, I had read and pondered everything that a king's palace could contain. That was known to be a fact and subsequently often served me well. I offered myself for the position and it was granted me immediately.

My work consisted of copying the sultan's signature, with varying degrees of embellishment, at the foot of parchments. It was not a very absorbing task and my ambitions lay elsewhere. But I took it on as a job and, when one's vocation is not to be had, one job is as good as another. This one even had an advantage over others: since only my hands were busy, my mind was free to wander. So I could dream to my heart's content and imagine what my life as a king would be like, and what reforms I would introduce in my kingdom in order to bring my subjects happiness.

While I waited for that day, initially, to my profound surprise, after such a great reversal in fortune, my new life was not displeasing to me. At that time Tunis was a sprawling green and white city, without real beauty of detail but bountiful and calm like a woman in the bloom of her years, its townsmen affable and its common folk welcoming. Life at the court was equally pleasant. Its king, Jonkey, was an obese young man of twenty-five, kindly and contented, who thought all year long only of organizing revelries and festivities. What's more, his optimism and harmless eccentricities were fostered by the grand vizier, who quite correctly thought that his master would thus leave the real exercise of power to him. Occupied as he was by his various pleasures, the young king gave hardly a thought to humiliating or punishing anyone. On the contrary, like many a man with a single passion, his only desire was to persuade others and share the object of his passion. We were therefore frequently invited to the royal table. I was hardly in the habit of eating much, but it made me strangely content to see so many rich dishes offered at almost every meal—lambs roasted on spits, pans of royal bread and hot peppery food, sweet cakes and fruit in abundance, so that I had the impression of living in a continuous enchantment. In short, though his obesity disgusted me somewhat, and were it not for a strong musky scent that barely concealed the odor of greasy sweat emanating from his person, the king's company would have quite suited me.

I even had a companion of my own age, D'hou, the son of Bologuine himself. He was a handsome, impertinent, and merry young man who profited shamelessly from his father's position and seemed younger than me because of his nonchalance and my seriousness. He was of an indolence that would have been judged extreme were it not for his tirelessness in enjoyment, ingenuity in varying the occasions for it, and insatiability in both. He might have been called cowardly had he not had the daring to risk his limbs in every sport. No harm ever befell him, since he possessed skill and endurance that were the envy of all.

When he saw me, he would signal to me with his hand from afar by raising one, two, or three fingers, which meant that he had made love once, twice, or three times during the day—with different women, it goes without saying, not that number of times with the same one, which would have been ordinary and nothing to boast of. It was not that he took pride in it; he did it out of malice, just to annoy me. Then when we got closer, he would shout cheerily,

"Hello there, you epitome of virtue!"

In short, he astounded me, annoyed me, and secretly enthralled me; he disturbed me, because he delighted in pleasure, without ceasing to be delightful in my eyes.

And so, in Tunis, I had everything—friendship, leisure, and security; despite all this, I was not happy. I was at the age when one believes oneself to be of enormous worth, and wants to give it all. Without expecting my position to be very important, I had hoped it would let me prove myself. But for weeks on end, I wasn't even called upon. Was it for inactivity like this that I had prepared myself for so long in the desert? I finally revealed this worry to the sovereign. He dismissed my anxiety with pleasantry:

"Young fellow, is it possible then that you are unhappy with the table and charms of the court? A person who is enjoying life desires neither excessive wealth nor even glory. What could he need? His mind and senses are satisfied to the full."

This reply embarrassed me more for the king than for myself. Simplicity alone seemed to me to qualify one for greatness; respect requires a certain distance. I ventured an objection:

"Is it right for a king to consider his own happiness before everything else?"

The complacent monarch pretended not to notice the insolence of it; he enjoyed the delights of conversation too and tolerated some frankness, for he knew that taking some liberty with him was the price of good conversation:

"Pleasure is, moreover," he explained to me, "one of the few activities that carry no danger for the kingdom: since it harms nobody, it carries no dangers."

In this he was mistaken, the gentle king. It is not enough to refrain from harming others in order to live in peace—one must inspire fear in them. Events were soon to prove this in a tragic way. In any case, even then, I was unable to accept such talk.

I completely gave up any idea of speaking to him about my great project. For in my heart of hearts, I could not hold him in respect. Even if he were a rose among thorns, a king could not merely eat and drink. I also wanted to be king, but for other purposes than that.

Despite all my affection for D'hou, to my regret I had to conclude that, with regard to him, too, salvation could not come from such an ally. He who in sport would risk his life ten times a day, without fear of receiving a dagger thrust from a jealous lover, or of breaking his neck on a vicious horse, refused to sacrifice even a finger for any nobler goal.

I had been weak enough to open my heart to him, when I felt a need to talk and did not know in whom to confide; he made fun of me as he made fun of his own father.

"Where will you be a hundred years from now, and what will have become of your empire?"

Obstinately, I repeated:

"I have to win back my kingdom."

"Does it really belong to you?"

"It belonged to my father."

"He wasn't able to keep it for you."

I lost my temper:

"Well, it's obvious: your father isn't a king!"

"He will be one, I know it. And when he is, you'll see, I'll behave in just the same way."

Today I no longer know which one of us was right. If I had been less ambitious, and had had more of a taste for the simple joys of living, I could have remained at Jonkey's court. I could have been happy there.

I could even have stayed near my cousin. I would only have needed a tenth of my present wisdom. But wisdom is a late-ripening fruit, and perhaps a deceptive one; even if, by some miracle, I had possessed it at that age, it would not have been of any use to me—you will see this, Sire.

In fact, despite its charms and advantages, the court of Tunis offered nothing of overwhelming interest to a very young man who believes that the salt of life lies in surprise and the novelty of events. Nothing happened there. Worse yet, even when something did happen, everyone knew about it right away; mystery dissolved in that well-meaning complicity of all.

Reacting to a somewhat lingering glance, I had fallen in love with a young lady of the queen's retinue, a noblewoman in her own right. My besotted imagination immediately showed me all the perils involved in such a conquest: I spent nights drawing up plans and counting my few allies in a merciless struggle, to the point of the supreme audience with the king, at which my head would feel as if it were about to fly away. The audience did take place. However, the king gently suggested to me a long engagement, in order to find out whether it was a question of true passion. The next day, in each pair of eyes, I saw everyone's benevolent amusement. That made the girl repulsive to me, and me ridiculous in my own eyes, which is the worst of sufferings at that age.

I learned from that incident that I was well formed, had trim feet; and that my countenance, except for a few scattered scars, the traces of old pustules poorly closed, was quite agreeable. When one has these advantages, though, they seem natural and of no special importance. Women surveyed me with interest. I should have been glad of it; instead, it embarrassed me.

Was I going to wear away my life in this tame fashion, I said to myself, while the world was being stirred by so many great purposes? But, on the other hand, how could I leave such a generous lord, such a hospitable court, and such an honorable if undemanding position? I was trying to make up my mind, when fate took upon itself to make my decision for me.

The fat king's passive good humor, in fact, had its drawbacks. Though it made life at the court most agreeable, it abandoned the rest of the country, beginning a few leagues from the capital, to anarchy and the sway of raiders who openly flouted the central authority. The kingdom of Tunis was a kingdom of puppets in the midst of a forest full of brigands. We led a delightful life in which, except for the king and the grand vizier, the most important figures appeared to be D'hou and Turncoat, an amazing little man with sparkling eyes set in a head like a bird's, and an imagination as tireless as the vitality of Bologuine's son. D'hou was responsible for the outdoor pastimes; Turncoat's task was to make every moment spent inside the palace entertaining. A small orchestra of flutes, viols, and tambourines, dressed out in yellow, crimson, green, or mauve depending on the time of day, played permanently in the main courtyard, and was interrupted only occasionally by the sad news that a convoy had been attacked, or that a governor valiant enough to resist the cutthroats threatening him had been assassinated. I never knew whether to admire the monarch for his leniency or criticize him for the results of his weakness. I anxiously wondered whether there was no choice other than killing with kindness or imposing order with its attendant cruelty.

In any case, as I perceived clearly, Bologuine, the grand vizier, was of that opinion. Though the king had the pacifism of the obese, his chancellor was ambitious and harsh enough for the two of them. This man who, later on, was to hold such an important place in my life, already amazed me with his stature. Almost too tall, with a large-boned physique held together by the muscles of a wild beast, a nose in proportion to the rest, a look of discomforting penetration in a face burned dark by the sun—he emphasized his unusual appearance by keeping his head completely shaved and going bareheaded even in battle or at the most official receptions, thus acquiring the nickname of "The Bald." I disliked this way of building up one's own legend. Until life convinced me to the contrary, I could not accept the idea that true ambition could be measured by such trifles. Actually, my antipathy toward him resulted mainly from his disdainful indifference with respect to myself. But at that time I was just a young stripling and had given no proof of my value, while Bologuine was almost sole master of the government of a kingdom abandoned willingly to him by the nonchalant sovereign of Tunis.

The unlooked-for result of all this was that the blithest of kings had the most daring and deliberate of foreign policies. The slightest frontier incident was the occasion for far-reaching diplomatic steps; and, when the adversary's weakness allowed, a rapid and exceedingly brutal response. Hoping to supplant the sovereign one day as a consequence of the disorders of war, Bologuine continually maneuvered to lead the little kingdom into warlike adventures. He was finally successful. As a result of a confused affair involving some pastureland, without its ever being clear whether it was the Tunisian nomads who encroached on the lands of the people of Bougia or vice versa, war broke out between Bougia and Tunis.

While this mild country's inhabitants, in sudden ardor transformed into lions, exhausted themselves in warlike proclamations, to which the people of Bougia responded by slaughtering entire villages, the king gave us the liberty to go to Kairouan to wait out the fighting. The king's generous gesture put me in great embarrassment. Naturally, I decided to remain at his side. But this war, which Bologuine had provoked, seemed to me an unjust one and lost in advance. Ought I to run the risk of dying amid the rubble of a kingdom that was not even my own—and thus seeing the memory of our house snuffed out forever? I was quite relieved when, a few weeks later, seeing my worried look, the king ordered me to go to Kairouan and join the majority of the court, which I did.

My act, although belated, was to be held against me one day; it has been said that I abandoned the master I had chosen by entering his service. The truth is as I have told you, Sire. It was the king's order and, in obeying it, I also had my personal reasons. However, I will freely grant this: it is possible that those reasons were not entirely good ones. Perhaps, despite my self-discipline, I was simply not yet ready to face the horrors of war.

In any case, events bore me out: my unfortunate master was quickly vanquished, his country was occupied, and many of his subjects massacred. My only consolation was when I learned that the ambitious and also perhaps perfidious grand vizier was numbered among the dead.

Returning to Tunis was now out of the question, exposed as it was to the initial excesses of the victorious army. Turncoat, who had joined us with a few other companions in misfortune, suggested first that we request hospitality from Thomar, the king of Tlemcen.

That sovereign, he explained, owed his throne not to birth but to luck and daring in equal amounts. When he was a destitute young soldier, a plot was hatched that almost claimed the life of the sovereign of the time. The palace had been surrounded, and the rebels sent in a few men under the command of a captain, with the mission of seizing the persons of the king and his faithful followers. Most of the courtiers and the king himself allowed themselves to be led away without resisting; the others were killed on the spot. Then, in order to escort the sovereign to prison, where his death had already been prepared, the captain picked out two soldiers, who pushed the royal prisoner with the tips of their lances to the exit from the palace. At that moment, one of the two men suddenly turned his weapon against his companion and killed him on the spot. Then, throwing himself at the feet of the king, to the latter's joyful surprise, he kissed his hand and offered to lead him to a safe haven. In that way the sovereign of Tlemcen, who one moment before had been in danger of death, was able to rejoin the troops that had remained faithful to him and soon won back his throne; the name of the quick-thinking hero of this extraordinary incident was Thomar.

What followed is no less amazing. When order had been restored, the king summoned his savior. Saying to himself that the man who had held his life on the end of his lance and had not harmed it would be the surest defender of it in the future, he generously made him his confident and prime minister. The logic seemed right, but turned out to be disastrous. Thomar remained minister only long enough to lull his master's vigilance completely; as soon as he had gained almost all the power, the army's trust and the nobility's complicity, he executed the king with his own hands and seized the throne.

"A man like that," concluded Turncoat "could not help but sympathize with the tribulations of an ambitious young man."

This linking of destinies amazed and displeased me: in Turncoat's eyes, was I merely an ambitious and unscrupulous fellow? I turned down the idea on the spot. But hearing the murmurs of my small retinue, reproaching me for excessive scruples in a desperate situation, I decided to send a messenger to Thomar (after all, who is perfect, but God alone?). It was quite useless. He replied to my request that, if I crossed the frontiers of his kingdom, I would immediately be arrested and thrown in prison. That was my first lesson in politics. Thomar in fact was only too aware of the risks of generosity. It would be better to address myself to less colorful allies.

On Turncoat's advice again, we next set out for Cairo, where Idris III, the Moorish sultan, was staying. According to our informant, this sovereign was seeking competent men to make up a future government. We arrived in early summer. Turncoat, who had accompanied me, had been right; in Cairo I received the best of welcomes; I must admit, due more to my birth and my few adventures than to the young knowledge of which I was so proud.

The first thing I found out was that, to my displeasure, this time I was completely unknown. Then I realized that my very obscurity could be made to work in my favor, if I only knew how to make use of it. The land of the pharaohs was far from Tunis; the war against Bougia had been rumored about, but only a very vague echo of it had reached Egypt. I had the weakness to let Turncoat and the rumors of the war swell the fame of my exploits, without contradicting them. Since epic is always impressive, I was regarded as a kind of hero. Was I in a position to reject credit that I needed so badly? Exaggerating a little, I described to the sultan's vizier my responsibilities in my most recent employment, the fat king's particular fondness for me, my suspicions regarding his grand vizier the instigator of the war, and my fears which, unfortunately, were soon after realized. I passed myself off as a combination of an intrepid leader and a shrewd politician. Finally, I allowed myself to remind him that I was a prince. And so, when I let it be understood that I would willingly accept a responsibility in the new ministry, naturally I was offered a position worthy of my standing.

All that was necessary was to return to my new homeland. We joyfully set out again on the seventh day of the seventh new moon. Despite the importance of our train, increased by the noble bearing of our sovereign, an air of festivity emanated from it for which I soon found the cause. In addition to the most essential provisions, Idris III carried with him a number of rare plants and marvelous birds, of which he was a great enthusiast, I learned. The colors of the former, and the latter's song gushing forth from dawn onwards, seemed to me the best of all possible omens for my own future. It was under these auspices that my political career really began. Avoiding Younous's look, I concluded that, in matters of this sort, it is better to let others assume that one has extraordinary merits than to be a beggar with humility.

At the Court of Fez

I had never seen anything as sumptuous and well-ordered as the court of Fez, at least at the time of my first stay there. The extent of the kingdom, the number of its subjects, their prosperity, the wealth that the central authorities controlled, made this state the foremost of its epoch. In their intelligence, the city's founders had chosen a site that, in addition, provided the city with an advantage unmatched in our parts: the main spring that feeds this city is located at its very heart, enclosed within its walls, so that no siege could wear down its inhabitants through thirst, and so that on most days its beneficial closeness provides them with a coolness in summer and a sweetness in winter that are unknown elsewhere.

One can easily imagine how imposing the sultan's palace must be in a country like that. What an amazing congruence of the prince and the artist! Only an alliance like that can make a mark on history! This is only right; for in it alone are summarized and condensed the energy and thought of an entire century. The sultan's palace in Fez was really the quintessence of the wealth and subtle beauty of the city in its best years. The magnificent building, located in the center of this site so well protected by nature, and girded with formidable walls, benefited from a certain freedom within its very severity. Since the artist had worked in the airy bliss of absolute freedom, his happiness expressed itself irresistibly in sublime unconstraint. Marble, wood, metal, which he had hunted down and bent to his refined fantasy, leapt forth, danced, intertwined, harmonized, as if they had become completely weightless; stone became latticework and the sky glimpsed through it seemed more solid than its frame, as if the artist had used

2. "At the court of Fez." Courtesy of Albert Memmi.

stone to make a mold for light. Everywhere, in fact, there were open patios, colonnades, perspectives extending down the gardens, fountains of water, delicate draughts of air subtly controlled, all giving the impression that one was sailing under a full wind.

Excuse my enthusiasm, Sire, for I don't doubt that your own capital encloses many comparable marvels, but you have to bear in mind who I was and whence I came. I might as well admit that, despite my austere attitude, I was impressed by the bringing together of so much opulence and grace, by the power and ingenuity of the human spirit, when it is not engrossed by discord. For, later on, how unfortunate Fez was to be!

Within the palace there was, of course, assembled in profusion all that was conducive, not only to repose and the body's comfort, but also to the delight of all the senses, the eyes, the sense of touch, and the sense of smell. Mosquito nets brocaded in gold and scattered with pearls; cushions of plush leather, sable, and lynx; luxurious materials, muslins from Mayin and precious stuffs from Alexandria; vases of rock crystal and silver; translucent porcelain from China; platters of lapis lazuli; and of tin encrusted with rare metals, amber, ivory, and ebony, all in abundance. All of these were carefully distributed in spaces proportionate to them, illuminated by small windows with colored glass shedding the refracted light, which recomposed itself marvelously as it touched the stuffs, the gold and copper, so that each enclosed space seemed like a silent fairyland; and so also that the entire palace, apparently open to the four winds, an immense arabesque in stone, at the same time hid within its heart, dotted around in a seemingly haphazard way, the most fascinating collection of hideaways of mystery and dreams.

You will agree, Sire, that one cannot live thoughtlessly in such a mansion!

From the day after our arrival in Fez, as soon as the excitement of return had subsided, the atmosphere changed completely. In essence, until that moment, we had all been traveling companions: a little confused, despite the size of our train and the opulence of our leader, by our mutual dependency during the trip, the discomfort of cramped quarters, and the unavoidable proximity in hasty encampments. During an attack by marauding nomads, the heat of battle, cries of the wounded, heroic deeds performed for the benefit of all, even created for a moment the illusion of a similar solidarity among the members of the sultan's train; individual rank seemed to have been almost forgotten.

We had hardly settled down in the court when each one, having again donned his robe of honor, the sign of his rank, regained his position in the hierarchy that thenceforth was to govern our lives. The most insignificant gesture, the slightest word, was considered and weighty, and I found that pleasing; strict formality controlled each of our actions, and that I found onerous, and also paradoxical, since we were the most powerful people in the kingdom. For example, the homage to the sovereign, which each of us was obliged to pay in a proportion decided in advance, began upon rising, continued throughout the day, and was not completed until the moment when he retired for the most solitary slumber. But we ourselves were each entitled to the honors proper to his particular office. Within my own ministry, I was treated like a sort of monarch. If I should sneeze, for example, I immediately provoked from my subordinates a series of approbations, encouragements, and blessings, in emotional and praise-laden formulas. All this was much too flattering to displease me and I took some pleasure in it.

In this court, with its venerable traditions, the art of reigning had reached its highest level. And I learned a great deal there. At one of the king's first audiences, a young guard came and complained of his captain, who had an excessively heavy hand in inflicting punishments on his men. He showed his bleeding back, zigzagged with many wounds, due to some peccadillo. The sultan verified the accusation and it turned out to be accurate. What did the sultan do then? Instead of remonstrating with his captain of the guard, whose services he appreciated, he first sent the young man to the dungeon to punish him for his impudence. Then, when he came out of prison, he had him made an officer in order to allow him to exercise authority in his turn. Such was the way of that great sovereign. He made his powerful wishes firmly known, but to each he gave subordinates; that was enough for each to endure his condition.

Impatient as I was to prove myself, and desirous of practicing my profession, I sometimes wondered, I grant, whether we were not spending more time on all these ceremonies than on working for the good of the kingdom. But—I thought, with confidence and respect—no doubt these were the notions of a mere novice. The art and pleasure of governing must include as much the artifice as the real exercise of power.

In any case, in Fez appearance was considered essential for the control of public matters. A guilty state official accepts a death sentence without flinching; touched by his submissiveness, the sultan grants that he may be executed in his uniform of office. I could hardly see the difference; I said to Younous that all the man about to be hanged needs is to have a sweet to suck on. I was making a mistake;

the man rushed to the sultan and kissed his hand, before being led to his punishment. Another time a minister and prince, having gotten lost with too small a retinue, was attacked by brigands and so thoroughly plundered that he had to return on foot, naked beneath a sack of jute left him by the mocking brigands. He crossed the entire city in this outfit. When he arrived at the palace, the sultan refused to receive him and immediately informed him that he was to be stripped of his possessions and exiled. In reply to his groanings at this double blow of fate, the sultan deigned to have the reply sent to him that he was not punishing him for having been despoiled by brigands but for having crossed the city without the insignia of his office; a prince without breeches is no longer a prince.

In short, at first I was dazzled by my new life; by the splendor of the palace and the air of grandeur that one breathed in it, by the magnificence of my new sovereign. Idris III, the sultan, was almost a giant, usually motionless with eyes half-closed behind heavy lids, sparing with his words, and from whom each of us nervously expected some short, definitive sentence that would overturn our life. Despite all this, he did not seem to be lacking in kindness, I thought, so I was waiting for an occasion to confide in him about my own business, when a certain event made me hesitate. A few weeks after our arrival, the sultan received a foreign sovereign with extraordinary honors. I thought it was the visit of a relative or a long-term ally. I was corrected, for he was a vanquished king; he had even for some time been a dogged enemy who had only been captured by surprise.

"What is this?" I said, "You do not execute him, or at least banish him from his kingdom?"

"No," they answered, "That is not our sultan's policy. Instead of killing or exiling the kings vanquished by our armies, which would not fail to awaken endless bitterness, he leaves the unfortunate enemy on his throne. He merely makes him one of his lieutenants and sets him up again as a governor-king in his own country, which has now become a new province of the empire. Seeing no change in their daily lives, directly obeying the same master, paying the same tribute, the inhabitants hardly think of revolting. The former king, very happy that more complete disaster has been avoided, resigns himself to a situation that, after all, spares his pride. Only the taxes change their destination, which is all we need.

Soon, I was apprised of even subtler strategies. Anyone asking Idris III for help received it forthwith: a king threatened by an unruly neighbor or some internal sedition, a tribe threatened by loss of its pastures, or a people in danger of losing its liberty. There was no need to send even one armed man: the formidable protection of Fez, once formally promised, was in general enough to discourage the assailant. But the price of this potential aid was to swear an oath of allegiance and pay tribute. So that in order to preserve one's life or possessions, one had to sign them away in advance.

That fact definitively restrained me from seeking the support of Fez. Under the pretext of winning back my kingdom, should I begin by giving it away? May the Lord preserve us from too-powerful allies! However, I could not help admiring that masterly edifice, that immense empire sustained by such an effortless system. Granted, Idris III only ruled it through intermediary sovereigns, but this very distance between the peoples and himself, all those crowned lieutenants, made him more fabulous yet and gave him the name "He-Who-Rules-Over Kings." Later on, in fact, all those princes seceded, as soon as the central power became enfeebled. Suddenly exposed as rotten to the core, the whole edifice collapsed behind its façade of dust. Even today I have still not grasped how such political perfection, such a powerful army, such a well-ordered administration, could all disappear forever. Perhaps everything, all of human history, has to be begun over and over again.

In the meantime, why was it necessary for such shining success among nations to be accompanied by such severity toward its subjects? Why should such greatness be sullied with so much cruelty? Unless it is that the prince's eminence requires that the subjects be downtrodden, and that therein lies the essence of a great reign and a great sovereign.

Idris III often preferred the pleasing simplicity of the gardens to the palace's pomp. It was in the gardens that the sultan, with his height increased by his tall headdress, dispensed justice in the morning in the presence of the entire court. I am still astounded by it all: there was such a contradiction between the sweetness of such a cheerful setting and the terrible decisions that were made there, sometimes affecting personages of the highest rank. The sultan had even chosen a permanent location for a second throne, beneath a large jasmine bush and facing a large fountain. Many rare flowers had been planted around. They were all beautiful, each more amazing than the next, and all brought from far away. White roses from Syria, red roses from Egypt, Indian marigolds, salvia, lilies and irises, all worked together to make that setting another palace of colors and scents. To please the ear, dozens of cages hung from the trees; they held the most skillful singing birds, those with the most melodious and refined voices—nightingales, ring pigeons, blackbirds, turtle doves, woodpigeons. Of course, many other birds chosen for their rareness and beauty, such as turkey hens or Chinese ducks, strutted freely around the garden. Amid all this greenery, flowers, and wonderful creatures of God, the king's chair was set on a platform encrusted with ivory, ebony, and other precious woods; and when the heat was overwhelming despite the coolness of the place, which was almost constant due to the fountains and all the vegetation constantly sprinkled with water, then slaves posted here and there would slowly undulate fans.

It was in this earthly paradise that an ambassador back from a mission was condemned to suffer the most humiliating corporal punishments; a financier was deprived of his fortune and his life, before having his head hung up at the city gate until it rotted. I watched a wayward official, an insolent officer, and an adulterous couple being judged, all in the same morning.

The official, an assistant qadi, was accused of having celebrated the second marriage of a widow who had not yet allowed the legally required period of widowhood to elapse. The sultan had the accused appear before him and without allowing him to utter a single word

3. "The Officer was cut in two before our eyes." Courtesy of Albert Memmi.

of explanation, condemned him to receive two hundred lashes on the spot, then to be wrapped in the innards of a cow, daubed with manure, and led through the city streets. He was accordingly laid on the ground and began to receive the first stage of his punishment when, on the hundredth blow, his heart stopped beating and he was spared the rest of his suffering.

The officer was cut in two, also in front of our eyes. It is true that this unlucky fellow, who had first been condemned to a mere beating for having allowed a prisoner to escape, had lost his temper and had muttered an insolent word which, it seems, was overheard.

The woman, a concubine of the vizier's harem, and the man, a black guard, had erred together. The sovereign occasionally made a game of consulting one of us: that day, it was my turn. The crime was not a terrible one; the woman was young and beautiful, the guard a magnificent figure of a man. But I knew that the sultan's unvarying judgment for such crimes, at least in the case of his own wives, was death. Should I appear to reproach him for his previous judgments? Who would dare to cross his king by vainly trying to save the lives of two wretches, one of whom was black? And then, what madness takes hold of women sometimes? Should not order be imposed with a firm hand? I obligingly said, "Death."

I saw with surprise that I had displeased the sultan; a murmur of disapproval rippled through the assembled court. I had obviously ignored some implicit rule of this cruel game. It was explained to me later that when he did not want to apply the customary punishment, in order not to contradict his own rulings, the sultan asked the advice of one of his ministers, who was supposed to appear indulgent. Then the magnanimous sovereign would agree through regard for the minister he had consulted. I was judged severely; since I was a foreigner, the criticism of some was lighter, while it served as a pretext for the harsher criticisms of others. I was quite annoyed with myself since, in order not to displease, or for some more obscure reason, I had been more pitiless than I would have liked. However, since the specifics of the punishment were always the sultan's prerogative, he condemned them to be hanged together, face to face. As she passed me by, the woman cursed me, which increased my regret.

In truth, I had just discovered the troubled pleasure that lies in judging and condemning, holding in one's hands the lives and deaths of others. It is natural for a prince to wish to preserve such prerogatives for himself alone. I promised myself to reflect on it carefully when my turn came to be king. Would to God I might succeed in bringing happiness to my people, without sacrificing my glory! In the meantime, I saw so many beatings, flagellations, compressions by the bowstring of sexual organs and limbs, doled out both before trial in order to make the accused confess, and after trial as punishment, that I could only bless fate for having me be born as one of the powerful.

During the rest of the time, all those handsome princes and high personages dedicated themselves to games of skill and bravery, since their condition freed them from all tasks and all cares. These activities, each more dangerous than the next, were often disastrous for those lords. It was not unusual to see someone ruin himself in a single night and be reduced to changing his condition or departing on some far-flung expedition, in order to make his fortune again. The games of bravery were of extreme roughness and danger. During my first stay in Fez alone, one gentleman was hit in the eye by a piece of wood from a lance and soon died of it, while another broke his back when he fell from a horse galloping into a fence that he had been unable to jump in time. The lame and the one-eyed are legion in the annals of courts, although chroniclers have an aversion to mentioning them.

I was surprised and amazed that such an easy life did not lead these men who were the darlings of luck to become soft, or at least to enjoy peacefully the privileges and riches to which they had been born, but perhaps everyone needs a game that makes him nobler in the eyes of himself and others. Princes already have everything; what could they play with, but with death itself, risking their own lives or having others' lives at their mercy?

I occasionally took part in these jousts. But I owned almost nothing and could not meet the bets for long. Despite my toughness, I was clumsy in physical challenges; my rivals, who had been trained since childhood, outclassed me effortlessly. Moreover, I believed that a minister should devote himself to his ministry, rather than to the pleasures of the game hall or exercise field. So I stopped putting in an appearance there. This was a mistake: it was taken as standoffishness and impoliteness. I soon had the occasion to learn, to my cost, that a reputation is built and reinforced as much in pastimes as in serious matters.

Tacpharinas

I took my responsibilities with the seriousness that seemed to me appropriate to the grandeur of that great court. I thought up important projects for my subordinates. I set up writing workshops, in which all the work of the pen would be centralized, where the chronicles of the various provinces would be written, and above all the sacred texts would be copied. A people's memory must be more truthful than that of individuals. Moreover, it would allow my staff to earn their own living; it was not a good thing, I thought, for men sound in mind and limb to have nothing to do with their time. I soon had to recant.

As vizier of the pen, I had full authority over all those who, by profession, sport, or necessity, wielded the pen: process servers, notaries, schoolmasters; and also historians and poets. The first group never gave me any difficulties. This was fortunate, since the second group gave me so many that I repeatedly asked the sultan for a change of ministry. He always refused, since I was there because of my reputation as a cultivated man possessing a good hand.

At least I had the opportunity to get acquainted with a quite extraordinary circle. Taking advantage of my facility in writing, I myself tried to record the main events of my life; I thought that later on I would give them to Sebbagh, our historiographer, so that he could reconstruct our genealogy without breaks. But I also realized how much my pen's obedience was merely feigned. It inserted fantasy so cunningly that, if I was not constantly on guard, it recorded as much fable as fact. And then I had to deal with people who not only permitted this confusion but prided themselves on it as if it were an outstanding merit.

One of them, a huge Libyan full of guile who was an enormous eater, invariably took two or three turns around the garden at twilight every day, with half-closed eyes mumbling incomprehensible sentences, which he said rose to his lips despite himself. Another one, from the Sahel, had such an imposing bone structure that he seemed imprisoned by it. He was perpetually glowering like death itself and claimed to be an intimate friend of I know not what mysterious spirit that he called the Power-from-Above or the Power-from-Below, I forget which. All of them, in fact, claimed to be the bearers of fearful secrets, of which I have never witnessed the most minimal effects during the two years I spent in Fez. I tried to joke about this with Turncoat. Did he also hold these beliefs, or was it that he preferred to abstain from criticizing such well-established persons? He was evasive.

Moreover, no one considered the behavior of my subordinates bizarre or excessive. In that well-policed nation, taste in the arts was such that anyone who had scribbled a hundred lines of verse or molded a few plaster reliefs was considered blessed by God. Moreover, he felt authorized by that to speak in a loud voice, and interpose his opinion in all discussions and on all subjects, a privilege that the court writers certainly did not forego. With assured audacity, they gave their opinions on the most complicated affairs of state and relations among kingdoms. The strangest part was that the king, who hardly deigned to consult with financiers and entrepreneurs, listened to them with kindly indulgence. Was he also impressed by their famous powers, or did he merely view them as his jesters? In any case, these tattletales found respect in the eyes of the empire builders. Perhaps the theater of princes has its corresponding theater of artists, as their mutual complicity tends to prove.

At the time I appreciated neither one nor the other. I just wished all mankind could be true to itself, and the great even more than the small. When I saw them together, outdoing each other in insolence and vanity, I felt overcome by vexation, remembering the old palace at the bottom of the park, far apart from the salons of my uncle the king, where the same comedy was being played out. However, as I told myself again and again, now I am a minister and I hope to be a king. I'll make sure, though, never to become a king of this sort.

Turncoat, however, flourished in that atmosphere. He had gained weight, so that his small stature, which embarrassed him greatly, was compensated for by his new girth. Though he still resembled a bird, it was now a nice, plump, full-plumed one. He had been a Christian who had converted as a means of escape when he was captured on the seas and sold in the slave market of Algiers, and I never found out how he succeeded in leaving the town, then reaching Tunis and the fat king's court, where I met him. He made himself quite useful there, thanks to his talents in the arts. I learned from other sources (since by then he acted as a person of consequence and hardly deigned to speak to me) that he had been the organizer of the famous permanent orchestra that played day and night in the palace courtyard, mingling itself with the king's waking and sleeping moments alike; it was he who had thought up the succession of colors in the musicians' garments, varying according to the hour and the piece of music. After the kingdom had collapsed, while I decided to try my luck elsewhere, he had wanted to return to Tunis in the hope of seducing the conquerors by the same tricks. I dissuaded him by depicting to him the dangers of this enterprise. He was no longer an auctioned-off slave, a man without responsibility, whom one buys without regard to his past, but the dignitary of an enemy kingdom, almost an intimate of the defeated king. He was running a real risk of having his throat cut. He was so frightened by my words, and so grateful, that he began to rely on me and remained faithful to me afterwards. For my part, forgetting his former disdain, I became attached to him because of his very distress and thenceforth gave him my protection. He accepted it as a matter of course, though he was older than I.

For the time being, as in Tunis, he had little need of it. Surrounded by his own little court, he seemed the real minister. He might have married one of the daughters of the chief inspector of taxes if he had not made the error of declaring publicly that the tax collectors were miserly executioners. And that if he had had the power to do so, he would have distributed gold with open hands to the artists, instead of extracting it from them. He had to be protected from the inspector, who had got wind of what he had said; and he lost the girl, who was ugly in any case. But his audacity, his obvious generosity, and the risks he had run, all increased his esteem and popularity.

"How do you do it?" I asked him enviously one day. "I have never been able to cultivate anything but my solitude."

"Listen to this story," he replied "In my country, when the divers want to bring fish from the depths for the prince's aquaria, they take a bag of meat with them. Hardly do they reach the bottom than they are surrounded with a cloud of fish, attracted by the smell and rushing at this unexpected prey. All our divers have to do is push the most beautiful specimens toward a basket that they have also brought along for this purpose."

"Men are no different," Turncoat said in conclusion. "Always carry with you a sack of meat; it is the simplest and one of the most effective inventions. Do you want to win the favor of artists? Give them what they are most greedy for: that is gold and flattery."

That idea struck me as unworthy of both my subordinates and myself. I told Turncoat that it was unjust to honor the most audacious and ignore true merit, when its owners have more discretion. He answered me insolently:

"Do princes have discretion? Nevertheless, they are the most honored of the whole nation . . . What do you know about justice?"

I persisted that at least I wanted to reward those who had the most enthusiasm for their work.

He scoffed even more:

"Do princes work? Nevertheless, they are the ones to receive the most advantages . . . What do you know about work?"

I was at a loss for words. But nothing would have made me admit that he was right. As I have grown older, I have learned to yield myself to less complicated sentiments, and to take people as they come.

In the meantime, I did have to admit one thing: that I was no more successful in the profession of minister than I had been in that of courtier. My workshops were not doing well: few applied and they were always the least gifted. I could never get anything at all out of the others, even a simple piece of writing for which after all they had been trained, while they constantly clamored for more gold and meat than all those in the kingdom who worked with the sweat of their brow. It was as if the least little effort threatened to ruin their precious gifts.

I could have resigned myself to the bizarreness and indolence of these people if they had found happiness in it, if I could have been useful to them in some way. But I have never known such unhappy folk. Whatever I tried to do, I always had to deal with anxious, exhausted men who spoke only of their constantly changing moods, and with such seriousness that one would have thought that the fate of the whole world hung on them. They were constantly complaining about their supposed slavery, as if they had not chosen that calling which they defended tooth and nail as soon as it was attacked.

The most extraordinary was a certain Tacpharinas whose poetry, despite my resistance to it, strangely troubled me. Why on earth did he have to playact so much when he had so much genuine talent? His face was constantly so serious, his forehead, cheeks and temples so permanently furrowed with numerous deep wrinkles, that it recalled the face of a mourner fixed in a grimace of bitter sorrow! Grimacing is a sin, I thought when I looked at him, for it involves deforming the features that God has given us. He must have sensed my disapproval and from the start treated me, his own minister, with a more disagreeable brusqueness than he used toward anyone else.

In the end I got completely tired of the company of artists and entrusted managing them to Turncoat, who did marvels with it. That was the best thing I did. Knowing them well, since in a way he was one of them, Turncoat treated them with that mixture of patience and firmness, leadership, and dissimulation, that one needs to have with children, and perhaps with all men, too. He wasn't rewarded for that with their friendship, but since he was not seeking it, he didn't mind not winning it. My subordinates still continued to visit me, going over his head, but curiously it was he who became the source of all their unhappiness. When they did not come to besmirch each other's reputations, they complained about my friend. To listen to them, if one put together the vicious opinions that they had of each other, they were all ignoramuses and charlatans. And the most ignorant and deceitful of all would be Turncoat, without question! Luckily, I gave no more regard or credence to their ideas than to their personalities, and they couldn't take me in.

It was lucky I could talk to Turncoat about all that. I confided in him, and made sport with him about it—how they accused him of favoritism, which was quite true, and of keeping for himself the funds intended for them, which was absurd, for my companion was prodigal rather than miserly. Turncoat told me in return that I didn't escape their cantankerousness any more than he did.

How could I care about them? they asked. How could I possibly understand them, the flower of Fez's intelligence? Was I not a foreigner, and a man with his own ambitions? They even questioned whether I was really a prince, as I asserted.

"But why do they lie?" I sighed.

"They're not lying, they're dreaming," replied Turncoat, in his extreme indulgence for them.

One day I lost my patience. One of them dared declare to me openly that Turncoat was enmeshed in a dark plot on behalf of a foreign court. It was probably an attempt to substitute himself for my friend in my favor! Since I did not have Turncoat's indulgent attitude I was revolted by this. Moreover, the treacherous one was the poet Tacpharinas, the best, the most skillful, the only one who was aptly called "Poet of the Desert." The Lord alone knows how this title, which he deserved, touched my very heart. It was too much; it was enough to have Turncoat banished if the accusation reached the sultan's ears! Oh what a bitter almond is the heart of the envious!

I suggested that my friend decide the manner of his punishment. To my amazement, Turncoat asked for the guilty man's head. I expressed my surprise; it was my turn to plead for indulgence:

"He is the prince of poets!"

"Yes. That is why he must be punished as if he were a prince—severely."

I could not understand this sudden harshness. I suggested to Turncoat some lesser punishment. He refused to agree.

"You would hurt him even more. A man who is hurt is an enemy biding his time . . . It's better to finish him off; heads are best cut off with a single blow."

I decided to have the poet sent away from the palace. This would be punishment enough; he would not find anywhere else for his writings to be heard.

I soon discovered how mistaken I had been not to listen to Turncoat. The whole affair took on dimensions that I had not anticipated. Custom decreed that the condemned man should feel public disgrace. Tacpharinas was led to the big square outside the palace, where the captain of the guard stripped him of his robe of honor before an assembled crowd, silent and resentful that its best poet was being hurt. It is amazing how a man can be transformed, as if he were immediately losing both weight and height, as soon as his elegant garments are taken off him. I felt pity for Tacpharinas, but it was far too late. He left weeping and, I am told, in a few days became destitute. Later on, the dismissed poet was always trying to harm me, as were his fellow poets, whose intrigues probably contributed to my misfortunes.

The king in particular was displeased with my decision. As was his habit, he respected my authority, but he refused to receive me alone to listen to my explanations. He allowed me only to bring the matter up at the first council meeting, but it was turned into an occasion for reprimanding me.

"I called on you," he said, "to serve not your own glory but that of the kingdom. You love virtue, so be it; but look at your subordinates—I have never seen them so unhappy. You would like them to be hardworking, courageous, and honest, but I want them to be peaceful, and to limit themselves to celebrating the greatness of my reign. That is the virtue that I expect from them."

I tried to turn to my colleagues, the ministers, for help, but all I got was their ridicule. I realized then and there that my zealousness, far from turning my administration into an example of productive activity, seemed a continual offense to them. Wounded in so many places, I gave up defending myself. That was an even greater mistake, since one cannot rival a king in pride and one does not correct one error by adding another.

I left the council chamber shamed and confused. When I asked Younous for advice, he just said:

"Idris III is a great sovereign."

There was thus unanimous agreement that I was not yet completely skilled in the commerce of men and the customs of the world. I wondered sorrowfully whether I would long be able to hold on to the privileges of such a high position.

All these matters, however, might perhaps have died down and, despite my misgivings, I might have finally accustomed myself to this complex theater, both tragic and comic, which was being constantly played out in that venerable court. All I should have done was learn to play correctly the role assigned to me, so as to live in ease and the respect of all. At times it appeared I might succeed. Without saying anything to anyone, and keeping up appearances, I limited myself to affairs involving my lowliest subordinates: schoolmasters and copyists, while even more carefully avoiding anything involving the artists. For their part, since they no longer expected anything from me, they ceased paying me that excessive attention and resentment that one bears toward those on whom one is dependent. But it had been written that I was not to remain long in the same place. Proof of this was given me by a momentous thing that happened.

Bologuine

It was then in fact that a character reappeared in my life who had seemed so distant and formidable during my first stay in Tunis that I could never have imagined he would one day be my close associate; I would not venture to say my friend, since I'm not sure this sort of man could be anyone's friend. It was Bologuine, the famous grand vizier of the unfortunate king of Tunis. Though reported missing after the last encounter with the people of Bougia, he was not dead. When he realized the enterprise was hopeless, he left the battlefield with a few faithful followers. Then he began preparing without delay for the counterattack. Tirelessly seeking gold and men, seasoning his troops without respite in well prepared assaults, offering to spare the lives of defeated enemies on condition they entered his service, he soon found himself at the head of a small army. At last, he could dream of winning back the kingdom of Tunis—for his own benefit this time. Having heard about the policies of Idris III, he considered it useful to secure for himself such a powerful ally. So he came to Fez to make an oath of allegiance. In exchange for the Moorish sultan's protection, he promised that if he attained his goals he would pay a large annual tribute.

I recognized him at first glance of course, but the astounding thing was that he recognized me, without hesitation. The attention he paid me gave me joy and flattered me. My self-esteem did not really need such assurances, for in the meantime I had become a minister, and Bologuine found himself reduced to the role of a suppliant. But such are the quirks of the human spirit! Because I had known the man when he was all-powerful and I was devoid of power, because he had hardly spoken to me more than two or three times, while all the rest of the time he looked through me as if I were transparent, his sudden affability, due perhaps to ulterior motives, provoked an almost ridiculous emotion and gratitude in me. He kept the same haughty air, holding himself upright and looking down his nose with the same severity in his piercing eyes, whose glittering blackness could hardly be met, and of course the same bald scalp.

Having ascertained my attitude to him, he described to me his plan and, while talking, showed a determination that fascinated me. As if it were unarguable, he finished by saying that he was relying on me and my active participation. And I must admit that I did not dispute this with him, which turned out to be a serious mistake. But when one looks at a lifetime as a whole, can one distinguish what was a mistake from what was not one at all?

I just asked Bologuine why he was getting involved in so much trouble, when he could mend his fortunes again at the side of some sovereign, any of whom would be happy to have such a man in his service. He explained to me that, although they were not his people of origin, and although he had reached the city only by chance, he suffered at seeing Tunis and the Tunisians subject to a foreign yoke. I persisted in asking him why, earlier on, when we were both living under the peace imposed by Tunis, he had nevertheless provoked such a catastrophe by pressing for war. He could have remained the powerful minister of a happy-go-lucky king, who would have ceded him most of the power. He explained that it was because he suffered from seeing the country so badly governed. He wanted to purge the country of all that was weakening it; he could not accept the internal disorders that the indulgent sovereign tolerated; and he had dreams of extending and strengthening the frontiers. Jonkey did indeed give him much freedom, but he had to use cunning, scale back his decisions, and soften his initiatives. In short, he had to choose between glory and the little king, and resign himself to never being his own master. He had let slip a telling word, I saw right away. If Bologuine had not sought to be both his own master and master of Tunis, if he had not pursued power even at the price of war, even at the risk of his life, he would not have been Bologuine.

I asked him for news of our former sovereign, the tranquil and kindly fat king. Bologuine told me he was living, with his conqueror's consent, fallen yet reportedly happy, on the Isle of Galita, a tiny rock off the Tunisian coast.

"He hasn't even tried to win his kingdom back again," Bologuine added spitefully.

That is one of the things that never cease to amaze me: the inability of a man with a passion to understand another man's, when it is precisely those creatures who should understand each other best. For is not pleasure a passion, just like power? Doesn't pleasure, like any other passion, exclude all other preoccupations? I told Bologuine, a little foolishly perhaps, that I knew at least three kings with considerable paunches; of course all three ended up by being thrown out of power, but they completed the rest of their days more satisfied, to all appearances, than the ambitious men who had replaced them.

Luckily, Bologuine was so unprepared to accept such an idea that he did not think it applied to him. He related to me the last moments of the king's reign; since he was talking of a defeated man, he deigned to be fair to him. He hastened to specify that at no time was the king despicable, as if he suddenly felt a trace of regard for his former master. Granted that he did not do battle with the necessary vigor, but he didn't try to flee, in order not to abandon the crowd of subjects who had taken refuge in the palace. On the contrary, receiving the assailants with dignity, he offered his own head in exchange for those of the refugees. He inspired such respect from the dumbstruck soldiers that when their first fury had subsided, they realized it would be more useful to exploit a living king than his corpse.

"One can hate a king, but it is rare that one can despise him," Bologuine finished. Whatever his origins, whatever his temper, a king acts and thinks like a king. The grandeur of royalty breathes its dignity into anyone who is enveloped in it. What other intoxication can be compared to that? Isn't it worth risking one's life for constantly? How can anyone prefer pleasure or even happiness to that?

Bologuine was not expecting me to answer; he was dreaming aloud for his benefit alone and was thinking of himself first and foremost. I was happy to hear, though, that pleasure had not debased the fat king.

The Moorish sultan, having obtained the necessary information on my friend, and no doubt impressed as well by Bologuine's energy and determination, finally conveyed to Bologuine that he deigned to support him. He would permit him to carry out raids against rebellious populations on the borders of the kingdom as often as necessary in order to enlarge and equip his army. I asked for permission to go with my friend. It was granted me without haste, for this was one more error on my part. They were already dissatisfied with the way I fulfilled my responsibilities; moreover, there was still some mistrust of Bologuine, I saw clearly. But I was bored with my ministry and, most compellingly, whether I wanted it or not, my life was already taking another turn.

We thus undertook a series of supposedly punitive raids. We devastated a good deal of land and brought back plenty of booty—gold, goods, and women; we killed many men who tried to resist. War feeds on war: the more we enriched ourselves, the more we fed our ambitions—broadening our field of action, we attacked ever more powerful peoples. Despite Bologuine's carefulness in the slightest matters, on some occasions luck almost went against us, and from this distance I marvel how many times our fortune could have been completely cut off. But it seems that fate had decided to favor Bologuine, for the moment.

Once a battle was only slowly turning in our favor, after having been indecisive for some time. At last, fear gripped our enemies' ranks and they began throwing away their arms in an attempt to flee. From that moment on victory was in our grasp, while we were exhausted from a long and terrible day. The affair could have ended there, but it turned to carnage.

Have you noticed, Sire, that, of all the animals of creation, only man gives himself up to useless massacre? Oh, that terrible moment when the soldiers, faced with a defeated enemy that is no longer defending itself, instead of showing it mercy, redouble their ferociousness, speed up the killing and thrust their weapons with voluptuous ardor into all the unarmed flesh! As if they wanted to punish what was once a threatening adversary for their own initial fear, or as if the scent of the blood and smoking entrails, instead of turning their stomachs, goes to their heads.

I saw some still hitting their victims when they themselves suddenly fell, as if they had been hurt in turn by an invisible wound. It turned out afterwards there was nothing wrong with them; they had just fallen asleep! Suddenly seized by slumber, they collapsed on the corpses and remained entangled in them all night long.

Two hundred brave warriors were sacrificed like that in a few moments, without any additional profit for a victory already assured. A few, having feigned death, tried to escape under cover of darkness. Our soldiers, having already lain down their arms and begun to prepare their food, laughed at this clumsy ruse. You would have thought their amusement would have spared those wretches, often badly wounded, staggering and covered with blood. But they found renewed energy for a cruel game they began: amidst shouts of mirth and applause, seeing who could fell the most victims with their arrows.

When not a single target remained standing, they went back to their pots and started eating.

I joined Bologuine in his tent and told him about the horrible conclusion to the day. He knew the story already; the scene was often repeated and he did nothing to prevent it. If the conquered adversary had agreed in advance to come and swell the ranks of his own army, only then did Bologuine restrict himself to leaving the field of battle. I asked him whether it wouldn't be better to avoid such futile massacres.

"No," he replied. "We would disappoint our own people, for the sake of saving enemies. If they had not wanted to cut off heads and plunge their weapons into chests and stomachs, these men would have chosen to be laborers or shopkeepers, not soldiers. I don't want to deprive them of that pleasure."

Although I didn't answer Bologuine, what he said shocked me. I, too, have killed many men with my own hand, but never unnecessarily.

I have never given in to that terrible voluptuousness, decidedly one of the most violent of all. Today, I am no longer sure whether I deserve much credit for it; killing was never my passion and no one is entitled to judge the passions of others. I also tell myself that, in order to prevail, one must hold men's lives as nothing—and I have never succeeded in putting victory before everything else.

It was during one of those expeditions that I received my first serious wound. We had begun a charge; we were galloping with our lances thrusting forward and just falling on the enemy . . . then nothing else at all! That was the last moment in my memory, until I opened my eyes again one morning. I was lying down; seated by my bedside, Younous was watching me intensely. I guessed that I was returning from the edge of death and was surprised at not feeling more fear. On the contrary, despite my fatigue and the damp cloud that still trembled before my eyes, I felt a calm joy like the one that women who have just given birth must feel.

They told me what I no longer remembered; how I had been felled by a blow, and then engulfed in the fray. At the end of the fight, which was luckily a victory, I was believed lost. In the opinion of all it was better to abandon me; it would have been cruel to impose on me the sufferings of the journey, which was exhausting even for sound men. Having few men and fearing counterattack from the enemy, Bologuine always maneuvered rapidly; as soon as the job was done, he went back to camp. But without discussing it with anyone, Younous loaded me on a mule and brought me back at the animal's pace. From that time on he had watched over me day and night, washed my wounds, dressed them, and watched over the course of the fever until I woke up, which happened eleven days later.

This accident in no way discouraged me from still helping my friend. For the convalescent, everything has the taste of fresh almonds. Actually, I was avid for action; as soon as I was in a condition for getting in the saddle again, I began joining Bologuine's men again with joy.

I had practically abandoned my ministerial functions. Although I kept the title, the real minister now was Turncoat. I wondered at the fact that the system established by Idris III allowed me to continue enjoying prerogatives that I no longer deserved. But one morning, completely unexpectedly, I was arrested by the sultan's guards and, despite my protests, thrown into prison. I did not find out why until long after: the sultan, who was having Bologuine watched, had learned that my friend had pledged the same vassalage and the same tribute to the sovereign of Algiers. This would have constituted a mere irritation for Fez, something pardonable in a man of his ambition, if Algiers had not been in a state of incipient war with the Moorish state. Moreover, Bologuine had employed the excessive ruse of allowing each sovereign to understand that he would make his forces available to each of them, that is, against each of them.

I was worried about the fate of my friend; fortunately, he was safe and free. They had also tried to seize him but he had been warned and never returned to the palace without sending a scout ahead of him to let him know of any suspicious developments. He was thus able to escape in time. I was less fortunate, or less mistrustful.

The sultan's annoyance with me was all the stronger because he had not been able to seize the principal culprit, of whom I was the friend. He held me responsible for the trick played on him. I was thrown into the most frightful prison in the kingdom, a damp dungeon without air or light, where I was kept on bread and water. With bitter irony, I remembered the dry, hot, open air and the marvelous desert light from which I used to hide myself for much of the day. I also thought sadly how Bologuine's dreams had collapsed, as he was probably in hiding with his meager troops, avoiding the anger of the terrible sultan of Fez.

I often almost lost heart; thank the Lord I managed to keep my dignity. The spectacle of Turncoat's behavior, the shame it evoked in me, and the futility of his self-abandon, helped me greatly. The poor fellow had been thrown into prison with me simply for being my friend, just as I had been arrested for my ties to Bologuine. While I questioned the grounds for my misfortune, and for that reason could resign myself, Turncoat felt crushed by an absurd and wicked fate. He wept abundantly, implored our guards, and assured them of his innocence. When he was told he had displeased the sultan, he almost died of fright. Having no possessions left, he offered himself to the guards in an attempt to obtain their help and prepare his escape. All he gained was to be sodomized by the entire garrison, then beaten black and blue. He remained for two days without moving, and his frightened persecutors took him aside to care for his wounds.

We might have been forgotten in that horrible prison and died there of hunger, cold, and sadness, if an important and unexpected event had not taken place. A few months after our incarceration, when we were not expecting anything more from life, they came looking for me and told me, with surprising respect, that the sultan of Fez had been assassinated by a murderer sent from Tlemcen. That was only half true since, as I found out later, he had been killed by his own vizier. In any case, the throne thenceforth was held by the enemies of Fez.

This event marked the beginning of those continual convulsions in the body politic of that great state, convulsions so extraordinary that, even from so far away, you yourself must have heard talk of them. It suddenly turned out to be so profoundly affected by a hidden but already chronic illness, that this occasion was all that was needed to sweep everything away.

I learned then how little gold and glory can help us when misfortune strikes! Do you know what the fate of the sovereigns of Fez was from then on? A little after I left, one of his *emirs* who had been vanquished by Djouhar the Christian had a sackcloth cap with a horn on the top put on his head, was shut up in a cage, hoisted onto the back of a camel, and led through the streets of Mahdia before his throat was cut ignominiously.

Kenoun, the last of the Idrisids, had his head cut off. On the day of his death, animals were seen flying off in midair, being blown away by a terrible wind; the earth trembled and the veil of the temple was rent in twain. Calm returned the following day, and Kenoun's head was sent to Cordoba to delight the eyes of his enemy, al-Mansur.

Should I tell you how one dynasty perishes, how another is born from it? Since the death agonies of Sultan Abu Inan were prolonged, and the struggle between factions was threatening to prolong disorder in the kingdom, the grand vizier decided, in the interest of all, to strangle the sovereign with his own hands. Then he placed one of his own men on the throne, since he thought he could control him better. But as soon as he was enthroned, the puppet turned out to be a real king, one who was firm and decisive in action. There was no other way to calm his zeal than to have him assassinated in turn. Since they mistrusted others, the vizier and his friends replaced him with a five-year-old child. They didn't gain anything from this new ruse; skillfully manipulating the power vacuum, a newcomer seized the throne and sent all the conspirators to the netherworld.

In this way five sultans were executed in a few years as soon as they had ascended the throne, without counting the unknown number of pretenders. As no obvious reason can be given for this decadence—neither the condition of the finances, nor the lack of prosperity, nor the weakness of those governing—we have to conclude that nations, like human beings, are irresistibly worn out by time. If they are not broken by war, they are condemned to die of old age.

The irony of destiny, for me, was that I lost nothing in all this upheaval. On the contrary, as the victim of a tyrant, I was seen as a political hero. I was immediately freed and cared for, and they offered me a position in Fez, although with a rank inferior to the previous one. I refused it. I felt it impossible, in a place in which I had experienced some glory, to descend in dignity. Besides, I had not yet quite recovered from my imprisonment. Above all, since the supporters of the deceased sultan had not lost all their power, I thought they might try to win back authority. I was running the risk of being guilty once again, and deserving it no more than the first time. In short, it seemed preferable to put some distance between myself and that place, which had become so bizarre that destiny changed there every day. A messenger having informed me that Younous was in Granada, where he begged me to join him, I went to the coast to look for a ship.

Before I left the city, I concerned myself about the fate of Turncoat, whom I had not seen again since he had been beaten by our guards and removed from the dungeon for care. I learned with relief that for some unknown reason he had been freed before these upheavals. I was glad for him, and promised myself I would ask him later about his most recent adventures.

Return to Tunis

I was convalescing near Granada when I received a messenger from Turncoat. Oh, what a messenger of good tidings! He was coming to inform me of Bologuine's coronation: for his trouble and in my joy, I gave the messenger a young white she-camel.

The blow that had felled his enemy had served Bologuine's interests mightily. From then on, he was free to act. Leading his small army in a relentless march, he fell on Tunis and chased out the people of Bougia. When my friend arrived at the city walls, the unfortunate viceroy, who happened to be one of the sultan's sons, had his throat cut by his own servants. As Bologuine had expected, he was welcomed as a liberator. Better yet, he took over in a way the legitimacy of Jonkey the fat king, even though he had contributed to his downfall rather than serving him with the complete fidelity of a grand vizier. But such is the strength of respect for royalty: it rubs off. In short, he was recognized as king without any obstacles being raised.

Where else would I be better received, and in more security, than with my former ally, for whom I had lost my position and been dealt imprisonment? I dispatched a messenger myself to send him news of me, inform him of the state of my affairs, and request his hospitality. I did not have to wait long. As I hoped, he answered me immediately that he was expecting me with great pleasure. Thus assured regarding my immediate future, I decided to rest a little longer before undertaking such a long and perilous journey.

It was not until the following spring that I finally felt able to take the road again with Younous and my few followers. That long stay in a damp dungeon, the hunger, and cold, had affected my health

4. "I gave him a young white she-camel." Courtesy of Albert Memmi.

more than I thought. However, the journey began with a lucky omen: we had hardly traveled half the way when we were joined by Turncoat, who looked in fine fettle and seemed completely recovered from our previous hardships. I did not recognize him at first; how could I have identified him with this imposing man, who approached us in an unctuous waddle, preceded by guards, followed by servants, and accompanied by pages? He had gained considerable weight again; he still resembled a bird due to his crouching figure, but a bird of a different feather: now even his neck, linked to the flesh of his chin, was no longer visible, seeming plumage which had filled out. He wore an embroidered turban of Indian stuff, a cloak of Djerid silk, a djellaba of watered silk and *rsacy* cloth, a silver knobbed bamboo cane, fine gold rings set with diamonds and rubies, golden charms hanging from a five-ounce triple chain. Lord, how clothes make the man! Even his voice seemed to have changed. We embraced each other and he whispered in my ear that I could count on his assistance. It seemed insolent to me, but he said it with such devotion that all I could do was thank him. From that moment on I rode along surrounded and protected by the equal affection of my two such dissimilar friends; the wary Younous, who as was his custom hardly opened his mouth, and the amusing Turncoat, who never stopped chattering until my head spun.

Toward the last third of the journey, we found relief horses, and provision of food and gold sufficient to continue more comfortably and without care. I also heard that officials, after providing for our needs and calculating the time it would take for our party to arrive in Tunis, were to leave at full gallop at that very moment to prepare for our arrival. That was the mark of Bologuine: lavish and efficient.

I was moved by so much solicitude on the part of a sovereign; and I noticed that from that moment on I rose considerably in my companions' esteem. I had not yet reached my highest stature, though. On the last day, when we awoke, we heard a great murmuring coming from the east, which would have worried us if we had not been sure we were already in territory ruled by Tunis. I asked Turncoat to go ahead and present my respects to Bologuine as soon as we saw him. I knew my friend; in that way, I was showing that I did not forget he was now a king, and I knew he would appreciate it. Besides, in the same situation, I would have liked to be treated the same way.

The murmuring grew and grew, and soon we saw an extraordinary procession appear. Instead of soldiers, it was made up of ordinary folk—men, women, and even children—who had walked for part of the night to welcome us at dawn, and would escort us all day on foot to the palace. At their head walked the king's representative, leading by the bridle a magnificent white horse that he invited me to mount. I did so to the crowd's acclamations. Everyone immediately rushed around us and we were in the midst of a human sea. These good people danced and sang with a joy that amazed me, since I had scarcely ever had the occasion to be at close quarters with a celebrating people. Between their ululations, the women chanted praises of the sovereign and his new favorite, your humble servant; in hymns of praise that flattered far too much the memory of our families, they celebrated the sublime virtues and fabulous exploits of our respective ancestors. I had the curious impression of having heard those words already, though at that moment I could not say where. The men, their fatigue obviously forgotten, jumped in the air or swayed in twos, each one holding the ends of a handkerchief that encircled his partner's hips; the horsemen pranced as best they could amid the swarming crowd, or went off for a fast gallop and charged back again; the children clapped their hands under my frightened horse's nose, or turned round and round, making themselves giddy just for fun; many people, both young and old, men and women, devotedly kissed our legs, especially those of Turncoat, who was the better dressed of us two and whom they took for the more important person. Before such a huge assembly of people acclaiming us, admiring us, blessing us, and making us the sole center of their attention, Turncoat repeated ecstatically, "Oh, what a wonderful show!" For him, that was the highest of compliments. And it was certainly the finest welcome I have ever received in my life.

We set off again. But we still made frequent halts; jugglers and dancers more talented than the rest went ahead and performed tricks and turns that evoked much enthusiasm; we had to wait until they finished, and then, like any multitude, we could only proceed at a walking pace. It took us over two hours to pass part of the Roman aqueduct, and then another hour to go round the lake that borders the capital to the north. Weakened by months of privation, I was also greatly disturbed by the noise coming from thousands of throats, the dust stinging my nostrils and eyes, the excessive light and dazzling glitter of the water, the heat that increased as the day wore on, the stench of human sweat mixed with that of the mud stirred up by the walking feet, the seaweed and decomposing fish; my temples throbbed and I moved forward in a cloud that obscured my vision. I was afraid of fainting, and I had to make great concealed efforts to hold myself upright in the saddle and stand the sun burning my head. Fortunately, the consideration of humble folk, which relates to humble things, is often as precious as that of the great. One of these good people, seeing my discomfort, was thoughtful enough to offer me one of those wide hats of woven straw that the peasants of the land wear.

We finally reached the edge of a town that I saw with astonishment was not Tunis, but a fairly poor village with houses of unequal size. It seemed to have grown up too fast after an event that one may easily surmise. There was hardly time for the eye to register its disappointment, though, before it was captured by and had to concentrate on a magnificent structure perched on a hill. Bologuine had thus chosen this mediocre cluster of dwellings for his residence, at the same time transforming it into a jewel box for royalty.

In a country with so many palaces, it might seem useless to add to their number. Nevertheless, the new sovereign's first order had been to have this superb edifice constructed in materials of perpetuity (of which, alas, only ruins are now left!). It was not that Bologuine wished to entrust his life and his government to the protection of a few stones. Naturally, he had more confidence in his own military genius and the strong arms of the henchmen among whom he lived, than in fortresses, which were all destined to be taken some day. But it was impossible to bring the new court to life in the pleasant places still full of the memory of the fat one. One only had to cast one's eyes on the new royal residence to understand how necessary the enterprise was: it was designed in Bologuine's image. As I have said to you, Sire, a true prince always finds the artist corresponding to him. Bologuine's palace was a severe edifice, whose elegance came from its uncompromising quality. Its formidable power, at first masked by the balance and purity of forms, revealed itself by degrees. It was simultaneously a tool of government, a fortified house, and a place of meditation. As for the town, he also had plans, as he explained to me later, to have it reconstructed according to his own ideas, naming it Bologuinia (alas, this never happened, and never was there any city bearing this name).

Bologuine was waiting for us near the first house of the village. He was also mounted on a white horse; a sensitive touch that affected me greatly, since only we two were mounted on horses of that color. Except for a heavy silver bracelet, which had been his father's, worn on his left hand (over his tunic now instead of under it, as he no longer sought to hide his origins), Bologuine still dressed with the same austerity. If it were not for his horse's coat to distinguish him from the other riders, the awe-inspiring way he carried his head, and the discreet deference of the men surrounding him to protect his life, nothing would have indicated to the eye that he was the king of that land.

I would have thrown myself into my friend's arms if he had made the slightest gesture or sign to allow me. But he intimidated me by greeting me merely with a slight gesture of his hand. I would have been disappointed with this apparent coldness if I had not already received so many marks of solicitude. I approached him and kissed his shoulder, which he accepted graciously in the sight of the crowd watching their sovereign. On his behalf, a page presented me with a robe of honor especially for me. I immediately put it on, to the cheers of the crowd. Then Bologuine indicated with another gesture that we should follow him, and in his wake we ascended the hill leading to the palace. The doors were soon closed behind us; outside the people were still expressing their joy, the muffled echoes of which came through to us for long afterwards.

A welcome warm bath awaited me; then I was left alone for a well-deserved rest in a cool, dimly lit room, opening onto a patio, where a fountain played. I enjoyed that calm intensely, I must admit. Strangely, those months of harsh confinement had increased my need for solitude. Before lying down, I prayed for a long time. I have always loved those moments when one finds oneself alone with one's Creator, and I wonder whether it is not for that reason that God requires prayer, for that daily encounter with ourselves. Why was Bologuine treating me with so many honors? He was my friend, and I was dear to him, or at least I hoped so. But friendship, however great it may be, is not a gauge for glory; it may even be the opposite. The answer seemed clear to me: I had served his ambition and, in his eyes, most surely, that was a priceless debt.

It was not till the next day that I emerged to stretch my legs in the company of Turncoat. The festivities, which had continued all night, were going on with the same frenzy of dancing, music, and singing as before. It seemed by now to have gone beyond our welcome and to be unable to stop itself. Some people who had not been to bed for two nights had collapsed, drunk with fatigue, and were sleeping against the walls; others, as if hallucinating, were dancing alone with a faraway look, or tirelessly reciting poems in honor of the sovereign. I suddenly recognized the verses of Shirazi, Jonkey's poet; the same panegyrics that had glorified the fallen king now celebrated his supplanter. I wondered aloud at this to Turncoat, and he chuckled:

Of course, that shocks you . . . Do you know the real story of Ibn Abdun, one of the greatest poets of these lands? As the bard of the kings of Badajoz, he first served the glory of his masters wondrously, and when the dynasty collapsed, he composed a sublime elegy comparing that event to a cataclysm. But when the mourning period was over, he put himself at the service of their conquerors, whose praises he sang with the same ardor.

Do you think the new sovereigns were scandalized by this? No, on the contrary, they prided themselves on having taken even that from their victims. Do you think that posterity has regarded Ibn Abdun's behavior as infamous? Not in the least: each generation garners his poems and aphorisms from the mouths of the preceding one:

Hast thou seen a Prince hurry
Or a Priest hastening forth? . . .

I could not resist capping this with the rest:

Flowers fade in their due season
And fish at their fixed hour
And death is always waiting at the appointed time.

Turncoat was right: I also knew the poems of Ibn Abdun by heart, regardless of whether or not he was a traitor to his sovereign.

As we strolled along, we chatted with the shopkeepers, who were lazily opening their shops. Once again I was struck by the cheerful and childlike good humor of these people. I had the curiosity to ask them about the terrible events from which they had just emerged, including the collapse of two kingdoms and the birth of a third, the exile of one monarch, the death of a second, and the coronation of a third. To my amused surprise, they told me that they had, in fact, suffered an earthquake, and on that occasion there emerged from the gaping earth some terrible monsters that devoured thousands of people. Thus, for them, there had been neither war nor defeat, but rather an accident that was not destined to happen again, and for which obviously no one was responsible.

As I returned to the palace I finally met D'hou, Bologuine's son, returning from a long hunt. Glimpsing me from afar, he ran toward me and we embraced each other. When the first emotion was over, he stepped back, sized me up at one glance, and grimaced comically:

"You haven't changed a bit! As for me, well, here you are."

He winked and made the sign with his hand that meant "Two." He was implying that he had just made love twice with two different women.

I teased him as well:

"So you didn't want to make your mark on history?"

"It would fight back and I would be the one to get marked."

We both laughed; he hadn't changed any more than I had.

I asked him how his father, now he had become king, could tolerate his behavior. He answered that he had not tried to find out, which seemed to me definitely the wisest thing. I was struck again by how light-haired and light-skinned he was, while his father was black, or nearly so, and had suffered so much from that during his childhood. I remembered how proud my friend was of having a blond son. Perhaps it was merely for that reason that the fierce sovereign, who had never shown indulgence for anyone, had such a weakness for this son, whom he liked to call "little fox," and in whom he pardoned anything.

Still amused, at lunch I described our walk to Bologuine. He answered me, with some impatience it seemed, that things had always been thus with this somewhat childlike people that had been poorly educated by its previous master. In that respect also he was going to put things to rights. I ventured that it was risky for a king to try to form a people in his own image. Then, in order to distract him, I shared with him my discovery regarding Shirazi's lines' having been adapted to a new use. This time Bologuine did not answer me. I had the fleeting impression that I had displeased him twice over and I wondered whether it was a good thing to speak freely, even with a friend.

Turncoat's Treachery

I was dining with Younous when I received news from my native country that made me very angry. It was a message from Sebbagh, our faithful historiographer: my cousin the king was razing to the ground the old palace where I spent my childhood; the old cemetery next to it was to be transformed into a garden, and the bones were already being exhumed in order to move them to a corner of the new necropolis; the royal park would thus be enlarged considerably. As for himself, Sebbagh apologized again; he was still not able to leave the country to join me as he had so often led me to hope; this time he had to see his daughter married.

What could I answer? What could I do? Yet more traces were disappearing. For how long would my people remember me? It is true that the palace had been empty since my departure and the old cemetery received no more dead. Oh, what misfortune is exile!

Since Younous seemed hardly moved by this new blow, I vented my spleen on him. Was he really concerned about what happened to me? Could it be that he approved of what the usurper had done? Younous, naturally, put up no opposition to this unjust onslaught; he only gave me a few rapid glances. Running out of arguments, I reproachfully reminded him of one of his rare promises:

"I will help you become a prince," he had told me.

What did that famous help consist of? To have me wait patiently until my own death? And why, it suddenly dawned on me to ask, had he discreetly said "a prince" instead of "a king." Wasn't I already a prince? Would it have burned his tongue if he had given me the title to which, after the death of my father the king, I had a right!

It was only then that he said to me, with irony, I thought,

"Many princes never become kings."

At least, that is what I thought I heard; but was I in a state to understand anything? My rage increased again with renewed vigor; I said stupid things of which I am now ashamed: I reminded him of his position as a servant and even of the color of his skin. It was not until much later that I convinced myself that he had said rather:

"Many kings never become princes."

And it was much later than that when I understood what he had really meant.

I have not changed my mind about his irony, though; obviously he was making fun of me, and my ungratefulness fully deserved it.

Bologuine suggested I take over the ceremonies of the kingdom; I would thus regain the responsibilities, as well as the privileges, I had lost in Fez. I declined, preferring, for a while longer, to lead an idle life. I did not feel entirely recovered from my fatigue but, above all, I was not in a hurry to find a new master; which would be bound to happen as soon as I took up service again, even with a benefactor.

Since it was becoming urgent to organize the first demonstration for the glory of the kingdom, I suggested to Bologuine that he entrust this task to Turncoat, who would perform it well since he would enjoy it. The king agreed, and did not have cause to regret it. The task was much more difficult than in Tunis because of the sovereign's temper and ideas, but Turncoat succeeded marvelously and was even entrusted with receptions for foreign guests.

One late afternoon, when one of these regular festivities had begun, I was obliged to leave the gardens, where the guests were, to accompany an ambassador into the palace. This official had expressed a desire to see a particular patio where there was a fountain of such perfection that it seemed motionless and made of transparent stone. We lingered on, admiring this marvel in which the artist had been so completely successful that the light, tricked by water, made the seven colors of crystal spring forth. We were returning slowly thence through the corridors, when we experienced a strange malaise; silence reigned, increasing as we approached the gardens, which turned out to be completely deserted. By some evil spell, everything had disappeared—the singers and dancers performing only a few moments ago in several corners of the park simultaneously, the servants running in all directions, innumerable multicolored lanterns, mountains of fruit and flowers, immense plates of food, cushions on which several hundred guests had been seated, all had vanished! The movement, lights, and noise had suddenly given way to stillness, twilight, and silence. All I could do was shepherd away my astonished companion, while apologizing for this inexplicable annoyance.

I wondered at this turn of events to Turncoat. He groaned that it was not at all his idea; he had had strict instructions from the sovereign. Every festivity must begin early and finish early, in order not to diminish people's energy for the next day's work. Every festivity must be luxurious and intense, in order to impress the guests; but every festivity must be short, in order not to degenerate into abandon, which is inevitable when pleasure is drawn out. Bologuine himself only appeared there for a very short moment, did not taste anything, and hardly opened his mouth; I think no one ever saw him smile. When he appeared, it was to indicate both the climax of the festivity and to signal its end. As soon as he retired, an army of servants hastily led the guests away, blew out the lanterns, put everything in order, and obliterated even the slightest trace of what had been an enchanting but fleeting spell.

I hardly saw my friend except from afar or in public, which scarcely counted. He devoted to his task of being king the same extreme care as when he was vizier, and I was careful not to interfere with his new duties. Twice a week he held a formal session to which I was permanently invited; but it was I who was far from eager to attend. The memory of the formalities of Fez was enough for my curiosity. Pleading my poor health, I was present as little as possible. And when, from time to time, it seemed necessary for me to attend, I found the same horrors there. In a single morning rebels were hanged, blasphemers had their tongues torn out, and petty thieves, who in their misfortune seemed happy not to be losing their lives, had their hands cut off.

Once, Bologuine specifically asked me to attend the reception for the ambassador of Persia. He had the dual singularity of being a prince and a blind man. I asked about the circumstances surrounding his terrible deformity: they told me that it was not an accident, but the result of a terrible order from the sovereign, his own brother. In that great country, in order to ensure the stability of the kingdom, custom had it that the eyes of all possible rivals to the throne had to be gouged out very cleanly by specialized executioners. Was it necessary for the requirements of power to be the same everywhere? Was it necessary, in order to protect the state, for beatings, torturing, and capital punishment to be constantly meted out, sometimes to the most honorable men, even those dear to the sovereign's heart?

Fortunately, whenever his affairs allowed him, Bologuine remembered me and sent for me. Then we spent a few relaxed moments in which I found my friend again and could air my concerns. I brought him the grievances of the court and the rumors of the streets; everywhere there were complaints about the excessive austerity of the kingdom. Hadn't Bologuine regulated dancing, forbidden alcohol, and punished, by death, the use of drugs? Hadn't he decreed that thenceforth the purpose of festivities would be not pleasure but national cohesion and persuading the people to love their king more? Without replying immediately, Bologuine seized my arm; "Come," he said, and led me to a pond full of water. They were swimming, crawling, undulating like snakes, those horrible fish called lampreys, with terrible eyes of opaque cruelty and supremely ferocious mouths.

"Look," he said, "These are all males; in other ponds you will find only females. Why are the sexes separated like that? The lampreys, which only reproduce once in their lives, die from the wounds they receive while mating. They are therefore captured before the mating season, thus depriving them of the act of love. You will probably feel sorry for them; you will say it is unjust. But should they die for that moment of pleasure? Peoples are like that," he added, "They are killed by pleasure. Believe me, a people that is too happy loses all its greatness."

I could not find a reply. Today, I would have asked whether greatness is worth sacrificing so much for. I emerged from these conversations disturbed, but not convinced. At least I learned through them to know my friend and what motivated him. These were the only times when he let himself confide in me a little. He told me about his humiliating childhood as the son of a small farmer, who was, moreover, a foreigner in the country. His complexion the color of medlar, baked again and again by the sun of the orchards where he had worked since his early youth, had not helped him win the esteem of a people that prided itself on its white skin. Even at the height of his glory, he was also called the Black Man, although it was behind his back; but things like that, you hear even behind your back. He had sworn that one day he would be an important person in the very country that exasperated him, and that he adored. He did not rest until he achieved his goal; he succeeded in being noticed by the fat king who, good-natured and lazy, as luck would have it, was ready to confide in a man he could trust. Bologuine fitted the bill so perfectly that in practice he became the all-powerful vizier of Tunis, even before the sovereign had thought of appointing him. His renown spread beyond the frontiers. Once, when he was on a mission to a foreign court, an elderly ambassador asked him if he were related at all to the famous Bologuine; he was only twenty-six at the time.

But what a road he had had to travel in order to reach that point! What tenacity and how much work, especially on his own self, had gone into it!

All those difficulties had sharpened my mind and hardened my will. I realized that I had to reform myself in every aspect; I decided to discipline myself in body and character. I had a loud and disorganized way of speaking which, when affected by emotion rose even more, rushed along, and zigzagged between high and low; I took a speech master, who taught me to lower my voice by several degrees and make it of even lowness; he taught me to control my outbursts and reserve them for rare occasions, when they took on even more relief. I used to let loose my anger too readily; I gesticulated, using my arms as much as my tongue; another master taught me to listen and wait, even if my life depended on it, until I had understood exactly, in order to prevent myself from responding too quickly, from which disastrous misapprehensions sometimes resulted. I lacked manners; I offended people by my impatience or clumsiness. I accustomed myself to laughing at myself, reserving my judgments, only speaking when I could do so without danger, making my body obey me instead of my obeying it. In short, I became a different man: the Bologuine that you know is the result of these efforts."

I admired my friend and felt a little sorry for him. He had attained his goal, of course, but what sort of a life is it when one imposes such discipline on oneself? When one assumes a borrowed body and mind? When for one's whole life one plays a role, even a glorious one? In order to dominate others, must one reduce oneself to servitude?

This is beside the fact that so much success had hardly brought him any rest. On the contrary, he had never fought so much as when he became king. True, Bologuine's military genius had him surprise the enemy rather than wait for his blows. But did he have to risk so much, and win so brilliantly, and as a result keep on putting his life in jeopardy without respite?

"Will the time never come when, protected by the might of your arms, you can dedicate yourself peacefully to your people's happiness?" Bologuine deigned to smile, somewhat sadly, it seemed to me.

"Where have you seen such a state existing? Was the lesson of Tunis not enough for you?"

To avoid hurting him, I refrained from telling him that his own behavior had had something to do with it. The fact remained, nevertheless, that the fat king's kindliness had not prevented the massacre of his subjects.

Bologuine continued musing, speaking to himself as much as to me:

"Look at the destiny of empires: it was never anything but acts of violence and pillage; the strong dominate the weak, while the latter does not rest until he can triumph in his turn, so that no one is ever sure of having won. History is made of shadows in which generosity and kindness are only rare flashes of light. Does that seem unjust to you and offend your sense of reason? The choice is really a simple one: do you prefer to be rich and threatened or poor and despised? You yourself, do you not want to reconquer your kingdom: how will you succeed without waging war? By violence and deceit?"

Once, when he had been detained near the frontiers of the country by an expedition that was dragging on, some thought he was having difficulties. The turbulent tribe of the Naccachi stirred up a revolt and succeeded in involving the Boutabels and the Mbareks in the quarrel. When he was alerted, Bologuine hastened back, leaving poorly extinguished fires behind him against which, subsequently, he had to begin fighting all over again. He could see clearly who the leaders were. But he knew that the Naccachi were too numerous to be completely exterminated, and too powerful to be put down without heavy losses. It would be better to have them on his side. The rebellion however had to be condemned, and an example had to be made, at least. Taking advantage of the fact that a few blacks figured among the insurgents, Bologuine had all the blacks of the region executed.

I reproached my friend for this.

"Ah," I said, "you'll end up by becoming a stranger to your own people!"

"What king is not a stranger to his own people? What the people want is neither a cousin nor a brother, but an all-powerful father; then they can have confidence in his justice, even if they do not understand it."

I ceased reproaching him when I saw the enthusiasm of the crowds at the public executions of the unfortunate blacks. Among the assembled spectators, the Naccachi were neither the fewest nor the least satisfied.

I was close to believing that power is the worst of all passions, when the saddest event of my stay in Tunis happened: Turncoat's treachery. Through what aberration could my friend, showered with benefits by Bologuine, enjoying his full affection, send information to Bougia? I would never have believed it if Turncoat had not confessed and if Younous had not also admitted that it was possible.

"Treason," he said, "is not simply a matter of money."

And in fact Turncoat not only admitted that he had done it, but also defended it boldly. He argued that he had not done it for money but because of his beliefs. He believed wholeheartedly that Bologuine was guilty of usurping the throne and of breaching both divine and human faith. Consequently, he demanded that he himself be treated with respect. He even requested a punishment, a light one it is true, but one that he deserved; and would accept nobly because of the nobility of his crime.

Bologuine showed no anger and did not try to refute Turncoat's arguments. He told him he believed him, but he was even more vexed for this reason than he was before. For if Turncoat had acted through desire for gain, the king could always have offered him a greater sum and secured his loyalty forever. But how can a man's faith be neutralized? Only iron and flames can consume it.

He condemned him to the stake.

Despite Turncoat's confessions, I ventured to reproach Bologuine for his severity. His first reply was a harsh one:

"The traitor has two eyes: it is not enough to blind him in one."

Since I could not deny the crime, I pleaded that this faithful companion had given in to a moment of mental aberration.

"It may be so," Bologuine allowed. "But the camel is the most valued of animals; sometimes it goes mad, and must it not then be put down?"

Finally, seeing my sorrow, he softened: "Death is not the greatest evil of all. Only suffering is shocking, because it humiliates man and reduces him to the level of an animal. Did I condemn Turncoat to one of the twenty-three corporal punishments? Did I order him to be impaled or to have his limbs torn from him one by one, so that he would be heard begging and screaming with pain? He will die like a man, if he deserves to; with dignity, if he is capable of it. I am only eliminating him to save the state; that is, for the good of a people. Should I jeopardize the life of a multitude to save that of one man?"

I could only bow once again to my friend's political wisdom.

By dint of prayers, however, I did manage to obtain grace for Turncoat, on the express condition, Bologuine specified, that he promise to renounce public life, and no longer try to play a role in any court of the civilized world. I went to announce the news to Turncoat, expecting him to be beside himself with joy; to my surprise, he turned it down. It was impossible for him to make such a promise; he knew that he would not be able to keep it. Political activity was as necessary to him as life itself. Nothing would move him and he went back to his prison to await punishment.

I was as disturbed by Turncoat's behavior as I had been by Bologuine's; I told myself that, in comparison with my friends, I lacked firmness. Bologuine's sharp mind and alert friendliness had, moreover, perceived this in me. I would remind him sometimes of the task that awaited me; the indispensable reconquest of my kingdom—if for no other reason, because of my loyalty to my father's memory.

"Are you sure you really want to?" he would reply. "One does not conquer a kingdom because of loyalty to a memory, even the memory of a father."

Then he would add directly:

"I will help you when you are ready . . . Provided, of course, that it is not contrary to the interests of my own state at the time."

Once, when I had had the same conversation with the fat king, the latter had thought I was thereby reminding him in a roundabout way of my birth, and that I was hoping to see my position in his court improved. He smiled, and the next day informed me that my financial benefits would be considerably increased. I felt hurt by this. But his fat man's cunning amounted to the same thing as Bologuine's lucidity. In order to reconquer my kingdom, first I had to want to do so. Power, like women or money, demands to be loved for its own sake.

The Queen and the Jeweler

And so one year went by. Despite Bologuine's insistence, I still did not take up any position. I rendered services, of the sort that only the heart can render; of that sort even a monarch has need, even Bologuine himself. I hauled D'hou over the coals, without much success, it's true. I explained Bologuine's decisions to people, something that, through pride and a taste for secrecy, he never deigned do himself. Above all, I listened to my friend and ventured a few pieces of sensible advice, which I flatter myself helped him a little. It is easier to give advice than to follow one's own common sense.

When he was still quite young, poor, and unknown, he had miraculously obtained the hand of the daughter of a notable of Tunis. That this beautiful young girl, with many suitors and a greater fortune than his, had preferred him to so many others had made Bologuine giddy with joy at the time. Hadn't she, with the help of her romantic mother, even circumvented the father? Being a man of a single passion, with little taste for women and their illusory diversity, his love for his wife did not diminish, though gratitude certainly played a role in it.

Unfortunately, with my friend's extraordinary rise to power, the giddy-headedness changed sides. The corn merchant's daughter could not keep her head from turning; she revealed an avidity that nothing could restrain and nothing satisfy. Jewels, gold, land, houses—the new queen seemed to have no other pleasure than accumulating them, no other care than creating new enterprises to increase her wealth. People talked about it in the land and even in the court. Wouldn't all that eventually affect the regime's reputation? But nothing restrained her; neither remonstrance, nor even threats, had any effect on the queen.

In short, every jewel has its flaw, and every man has a weak spot. Bologuine's was his wife. It was during my first stay with Bologuine that public scandal flared up. One of the most famous and richest jewelers of the city suddenly disappeared, taking with him an inestimable collection of jewels. Public rumor immediately accused the queen. The unlucky man had even, before leaving his shop, told his employees that he was going to show the fabulous jewels to a person of the highest rank. Whoever could have inspired such confidence in the jeweler? Whoever could have seemed to him a possible purchaser for such a treasure? And whoever would have dared commit such a crime unless assured of relative impunity?

But this time it was really too much: the royal mission, which was dear to Bologuine above all else, was in danger of being compromised. However much he was going to suffer from it, the king decided to repudiate his wife. The two of us were eating alone together, as we use to do sometimes, when he told me. He seemed so overwhelmed by what he believed to be this necessary course that I dared to pursue the subject further with him and discuss his action. He encouraged me, even soliciting my opinion on his decision. Instead of answering him directly, I told him the following story:

Having seen a beggar woman of great beauty during a walk, a certain sultan fell so desperately in love that he decided to make her his wife. He had her brought to the palace then and there, dressed her in gold and silk, showered her with all the possessions in the world, and after that not a week passed without his giving her some present. Of course, that aroused bitterness and jealousy, especially among the noble families of the kingdom, who could never forgive the former beggar woman for having been chosen over their daughters. No word, no look of the new queen was spared from endless commentaries; people rivaled each other in slandering her in every way. But besides being beautiful she was of irreproachable sweetness, pleasantness, and virtue. And the king congratulated himself more and more on such a fortunate choice.

"One day, a lackey, who was spying for her enemies, thought he had found a way to discredit the young woman in the august husband's eyes. Very early one morning, when he was on his way to the kitchens to fetch his service, the lackey saw the queen making her way, with all sorts of precautions, to an uninhabited little room far from the royal apartments. Following her, he noted also that she locked herself in with a double lock. There was no doubt, he thought, that she must be indulging in some sinful activity together with an accomplice. Otherwise, what would the queen be doing in that place at an unaccustomed hour for a sovereign?

"He thus went to present his report to those who were paying him; and these latter hastened to alert the king, with a joy that can be guessed at.

"Troubled, despite the confidence he had in his wife, the sultan wanted to set his mind at rest. The next day, having posted himself in the corridor leading to the suspect chamber, he soon actually saw the queen enter and then lock herself in carefully. The queen's treachery no longer left any room for doubt in the king's mind. Crazed with pain and losing control of himself, he flung himself at the door and began to beat on it with his bare fists. Since the occupants seemed hardly in a hurry to open, in utmost fury he started shouting: 'Open up, you infamous woman! I am the king, your husband! I want to take you to the executioner myself! Open up!'

"Finally, the door opened. The queen appeared, still in disarray, having obviously just dressed again in hurry. Throwing her aside, the king rushed inside to seize the accomplice. But he pulled up in astonishment when he saw the room was empty, the only way out of it being a high, narrow sky-light, through which no man could have escaped.

"Recovering his temper somewhat, but perplexed, the king demanded that the queen explain herself. The poor woman, trembling, not yet able to speak, pointed at a pile of objects on the floor in the room's semi-darkness, and which the king could barely make out: some crusts of bread and a few rags;

"'Pull yourself together, Madam,' the king insisted, 'and explain to me what all of this means.'

"'Sire,' said the queen, 'I am not doing anything wrong, you can see for yourself. How could I have betrayed you? You have made a queen of me; you have showered me with honors and riches! But do you want to know why I come here each day and shut myself up in this dark little room? I will explain: far from disdaining your goodness, on the contrary, it is in order never to forget the extent of my good fortune: every morning, in fact, I come and put on again my old clothes for a moment and eat a piece of dry bread.'

"Moved, the king embraced his wife and led her back to her apartments himself. He lavished twice as much care and love on the queen and announced that thenceforth he would behead any slanderer.

"Sire, I have told you this story as I have heard it; hear it with your ears. The Lord alone knows what goes on in the depths of a soul."

Bologuine had listened to me with the greatest attention; toward the end he became more and more tense, and as soon as I had spoken the last sentence he rose and hardly bidding me farewell, left me brusquely.

That evening, however, he came to me and thanked me for my parable as if he had just heard it.

"So," he said, "in your opinion, my wife is not guilty; it is simply that she has not forgotten her father's corn trade . . . But why did you not tell me your opinion more frankly?"

"Sire," I said, "it was difficult enough for you to hear it without anger, even enveloped in a fable with fictional characters! What would have happened to our friendship if I had given you the truth directly? Few men can listen calmly to something which is uncomfortable for them. Besides, what proof do you have of the queen's guilt, other than bits of gossip? Are you going to tarnish irrevocably the memory of your beloved companion?"

Bologuine finally smiled and said to me that, far from jeopardizing our mutual attachment, my advice would be followed; he told me that he was pardoning the queen yet again.

I congratulated myself for my contribution to this happy conclusion for the queen and for my friend, who could continue to enjoy the woman whom he loved despite everything. Moreover, after this alarm, which had been more serious than the others, the queen seemed to settle down. Alas, events were soon to render all these efforts quite in vain.

You will see, Sire, how tenacious evil gossip is. Today, when only ruins of Bologuine's palace remain, the few inhabitants of that desolate place tell a strange story to the few visitors. In support of what they say, they show a sort of cavity in a wall, in which the jeweler is said to have been walled up alive, and where the wreckers discovered his skeleton. These imaginative people even tell in detail the agonies of that unfortunate man, entreating, screaming as the wall rose up implacably, until his terrible laments were stifled forever.

Bologuine's recurring political problems finally obliged me to leave my idle retirement. In order to help my friend, I had to agree to go as ambassador to the king of Castile, Pedro the Cruel.

One would have expected that the order established by Bologuine, based on internal equilibrium and inspiring a healthy fear in the neighbors, would have lasted a long time. But there's no rest for the ambitious. Even when they finally decide to leave the world in peace, the world begins to trouble their rest. I do not know whether Bologuine still wished for war, but war continued to hound him.

The nomads in the far provinces were beginning to harass the sedentary folk again, devastating harvests, carrying off livestock, and killing those who resisted. Bologuine had to send repeated punitive expeditions; he came down hard on them, imposing on the pillagers a heavy tribute, double what had been taken, in order to restore part of it to the victims and recompense the army. But who can ever be sure, when dealing with nomads, that he has reached the real perpetrators? Whatever happens, they protest their innocence and whatever happens, they do it again. Bologuine even wondered whether he should not give them a final choice: to be exterminated or to be permanently settled on the land; it would amount to obliging them to disappear.

For a nomad, settling down was a no less tragic fate than war to the death. In any case, it was a long-term affair, a running sore on the kingdom's flank.

At other times, either sure of his strength, or already secretly tired, Bologuine in contrast put all his skills into economizing arms and men. Some echo must have reached you of the great revolt of the Majnouni, who seemed as if they would trouble all these parts without respect for frontiers. A poisoned wind had begun to blow across our lands; farmers, craftsmen who seemed to have been dozing for eternity, with their noses in their ploughs or workbenches, had suddenly put on the lion's coat. Declaring themselves the missionaries of a new faith, that they claimed was the oldest but tarnished by custom and sinners, borne along through space by the irresistible energy of certainty, their numbers grew as they progressed, striking fear in all the kingdoms around, some of which collapsed at the first engagement, or even the mere announcement that they would soon arrive.

A few years before, Bologuine's impatient pride would have made him pounce on that despicable rabble. Instead of trying to contain such a formidable thrust, which he could certainly have stopped, but which would have left him falling exhausted on the corpses of his assailants, Bologuine had an idea of political genius. As soon as the horde crossed the borders of the kingdom, and the panicking peasants flowed toward the fortified towns, he dispatched several emissaries to greet the principal heads of the bands. He informed them that he had been expecting them, that he welcomed them, and sincerely wished to increase his own glory by joining with the triumph of the true faith. He thus entreated them to accept his own contribution of provender, arms, and gold. It was a masterly stroke: flattered by this formal recognition by a king, their delirium calmed, they paused only to set up their tents for a few days, and then rushed off again southwards. Soon, when the unaccustomed wind had finally subsided, those terrifying combatants became as peaceable and harmless as leaves suddenly dropped by a storm. To their misfortune, it took not much time before their final destiny was realized: in vengeance or fear, so many were massacred that few returned to their villages. Likewise, it is true, the camel that tries to look over its hump breaks its neck. However, despite Bologuine's ingenuity, it had been necessary to feed those multitudes, give them all the equipment that they lacked, empty the treasury, and make great inroads into the reserves. The country was prostrated, as if a cloud of locusts had passed; not a single tree bore fruit, not a single blade of grass still grew. Most importantly, once again, everything had almost been lost.

That was not the worst of it: the foreign enemy still had not disarmed. The people of Bougia were motivated by the most tenacious and absurd passion in politics: they bore a grudge. They had never forgiven Bologuine for the death of their young prince, strangled by his servants, surely at the instigation of my friend's spies. As if they had not done the same sort of thing when they had bribed the unfortunate Turncoat! They insisted on calling Bologuine the Usurper, without remembering that they themselves had previously wrested the throne of Tunis from its legitimate sovereign, the fat king. But such are the laws of forgetfulness: one only remembers what one wants to. Bologuine was sure of his army, himself, and his country but, as was his habit, he wanted to leave nothing to chance. He had heard that the sultan of Bougia was busy contracting new alliances and seeking the support of a fleet. So he asked me to go to Castile, which was then a sea power, to assess the intentions of Pedro the Cruel, the reigning king at the time.

Pedro the Cruel was a Christian, it was true, and that could create difficulties. A shared faith makes for more natural alliances, unifies combatants, bolsters their courage, and allows them to die without worrying too much about the hereafter. But it is interest that moves empires; if we ourselves did not make this alliance with the infidels, our enemies would do it instead.

Bologuine gave me a large and splendid escort, to honor me and impress the Castilians (I don't think it actually had a good effect on them; rather, such pomp irritated the touchy pride of Castile's ruler; however, it did oblige him to treat me as a man endowed with such

5. "He asked me to go to Castile." Courtesy of Albert Memmi.

a following would expect). In order not to traverse the territory of Bougia, I would have had to go quite a long way south. Although I could then have made use of my familiarity with the desert, in order to shorten the journey I decided to go by sea. Of course we would pass the coasts of Bougia but, at sea as in the desert, one sees the enemy approaching from a long way off. So on the first day of summer, I embarked with my men in two swift vessels.

Those were days of enchantment and continuous reverie, as they are whenever I find myself at sea. As the coastline receded and diminished before my eyes, my need to trust in the sky and the elements made problems on land appear pathetic and their customary agitation so vain. It is true that I was on a mission to a powerful sovereign and was sent by another prestigious one. But what did all their glory amount to, compared with that of the kings of Babylon? What was the state of Tunis, or that of Castile, compared to the Macedonian empire or the Persian! Why shouldn't I head for other parts of the world and savor all those fabled lands? Our admiral, navigating with skill, kept us as far as possible from the coast of Bougia and brought us toward Algiers. We continued along the Moorish coasts and soon were in sight of Gibraltar. One month to the day after our departure, we reached Castile.

At the Court of Castile

I have rarely encountered a people as somber and ill at ease as the Castilians; at least, that is what I thought in the beginning. Even their blind men, who elsewhere are the most resigned of the infirm, are impatient; I have seen some of them knocking the ground with their sticks, cursing both fate and mankind, as if their misfortune had not been willed by heaven.

On the day after our arrival, the grand vizier invited us to a meal in our honor, during which he already began speaking of our business. Not being fully recovered from the fatigue of the journey, I heard him out with difficulty; then I made signs that I wished to retire for the siesta. I received reproachful looks; there was still much to say and the vizier liked to finish dealings of this sort as quickly as possible. I could not understand this haste; isn't the mind much clearer away from meals? I assumed at first that it was a ruse to profit from my drowsiness; this was confirmed when after this exhausting session we were kept waiting for three days before resuming our talks.

As for the king himself, we did not see him for the whole of the first week. When he deigned to receive us, he seemed distracted and appeared almost bored by my statements. He got up several times to go and kiss the glass of a small gold and pearl-encrusted cabinet containing, as I found out later, a few fragments of a human tibia bone; when he was not doing that, he was piously fingering either a rosary or a medallion that hung about his neck. Since ruse is not worthy of kings, but rather of viziers, I concluded from this that Pedro the Cruel, like his prime minister, wanted to convey to us that the Castilians have nothing but disdain for material concerns.

We were soon able to verify that this punctilious pride was a trait common to the entire nation. While the people of Tunis lived in excessive simplicity, making them ill-equipped for times of danger, the Castilians exhibited an irascible pride that showed itself at every moment and in everything. A people of small stature, all Castilians—I mean even the men—wear high heels and broad belts of leather or fabric, tightened until they are being stifled, obliging them to throw out their chests and hold themselves stiffly in order to appear taller; the women add a skillful construction of hair, crowned in addition with excessively high combs. I have seen some of them, noblemen as well as common folk, killing each other for an insult or an insolent glance directed at a woman. Taking the life of another, or losing one's own for some trifle, is part of their idea of honor.

One morning, as I came out of the palace with a few of my advisers, I saw a large, silent crowd assembled on both sides of the street, watching a funeral procession pass. They replied to our questions that it was the procession of the god of the Spaniards. It seemed an amusing idea to us that a god could be taken for a walk. But our mood changed when we were able to make our way to the procession itself: a plaster statue representing a man lying on a litter, carried by men who walked until they were exhausted. It represented a corpse, perhaps a decomposing one, since it was livid and blotched with thousands of small sores, from which drops of blood and pus were dripping. Funereal music and lamps veiled in black accompanied the sinister cortege. Although that god was not mine, it made me shiver; how pagan and cruel such a people must be to represent their Creator thus!

That disdain for life, that secret penchant for death, can be found even in their games. We were treated with all the respect due illustrious foreigners, and as a matter of course were invited to all the diversions of the court. I have already told you, Sire, how little I cared for such festivities. They were always the same: competitions in which vanity, ruse, and violence were pitted against each other. Since being in Fez I had finally acquired enough skill not to draw attention to myself, but that had hardly diminished my lack of interest. I continued to believe the nobility and worth of a man cannot be found in such contortions, especially if they are of no usefulness whatsoever. It was something else altogether in Castile. During my journeys, which by then were many, I had witnessed ram-fights, cockfights, and even dogfights; I had never seen a dual to the death between man and bull. It is said that in ancient times the Rumis made gladiators fight against wild beasts, but they were men meant for sacrifice, applauded like actors and despised like them. At the court of Castile, it was considered such a glorious feat, that the most respected of men entered the arena with the monster chosen for its ferociousness. Even the king did not refuse to go in person and plant a dart in the flesh of man's dark adversary. It seemed to me highly undignified that men of the highest rank should thus exhibit themselves, confronting an animal in public, using their hips, arms, and heads; then, when all this dancing and strutting were over, running as fast as their legs would take them to hide behind wooden fences. As for the poor beast, it would always succumb to the same cruel and wicked end: a sword thrust into the back of its neck, and inevitable death. When the blow was not aimed well, it was worse; then a terrible slaughter took place, as the man, incensed by his own clumsiness, fell furiously on his victim, which refused to die.

In summary, everything at first struck me as disproportionate, strange, and irritating, so I decided to shorten such a disagreeable stay as much as I could. How did all of that transform itself, in my eyes at least, into the very opposite? How did the ridiculous become simplicity itself, and cruelty become courage? How did a sinister reality become a golden dream? I cannot explain it to you, Sire, any more than I have been able to explain it to myself. I only know that it is in the midst of that people, who displeased me so much, that such an unexpected event took place, for the first time in my life: I became passionately attached to a woman.

Oh woman, that warmth favoring all germination! But I forbade myself excessive or too assiduous frequenting of women. It was not that I did not enjoy them; it has happened that I, like D'hou, would enjoy two or three women in the same day; but as soon as I had taken pleasure, I left them. That too had been taught me by the man of the desert: "Use or abuse women, as your temperament dictates," Younous had said to me, "But after love, then return to your couch, for you should sleep alone."

I had thus acquired that comfortable wisdom that men pass on to each other in all the countries where I have been. I knew that woman is the best of all intoxicants; and for that very reason it is better not to exceed the use of more than one woman a day; it is better to abstain for one day a week; if one takes pleasure more than four times, one enters a dangerous dizziness where one thinks one can reach a hundred, without exhaustion even entering one's mind; and that though blonds look better, brunettes feel better.

To these simple rules, I had added one of my own invention, adapted to my own use: avoid any involvement with the ladies of the court. I had heard that many men have made their careers there by being led with a woman's hand. I found that despicable and dangerous, for a woman almost always belongs to someone; also deceit, greed, jealousy, resentment, all those powerful emotions that women awaken, can be the source of great embarrassment. As a foreigner I already had the difficulties of my situation, so why should I add to them others that were avoidable?

All of this is to tell you, Sire, that thanks to Younous and my natural prudence, I believed I had conquered such disturbances in advance. I had no thought of becoming involved with a woman, and least of all in such a foreign court. Then I met Dolores. Dolores—my sorrow, as her name translated in our language—was first just a girl gathering flowers in the king's gardens. Her light blue eyes, the color of the sky, and her black hair with amber lights, surprised me in their unexpected harmony; her flesh, of a bluish whiteness, made me shiver in a way that I am not even sure was pleasurable; the face of a child crowning ample curves, as all men like women to be. She saw me, too, and perhaps because of my clothes, perhaps because the ambassador of such a faraway country had already aroused her curiosity, she did not lower her eyes. Her liberty shocked and enthralled me; I greeted her and she smiled at me; I had already been caught.

Why should this woman, among all others, seize my regard so violently and make my heart stop? I had never seen her before and we did not say anything to each other. Did she remind me of another who had inspired such emotion in me? Or was it just another case of the arrow of desire and the illusion it suggests? It seems that from that first moment Dolores had given me the desire to have sons and grandsons from her. I did not fail to see at that same moment the difficulties of the enterprise—for enterprise there already was! But what arguments I invented right away in response to them! Hadn't my turn come to do my duty to ensure our lineage? At fifteen, Dolores was already broad-hipped and well-made for childbearing without excessive pain, which augured well for the charm and health of my future children. And what better guarantee for a happy union, than that call of instinct?

That very evening, I collected information: she was a cousin of the royal family, but a quite distant one, and only of the queen. However, she was the protégée and almost the daughter of Pedro the Cruel. It was true that I was a prince; but one who lacked kingdom and subjects, and with no one to vouch that one day I would regain my right. If, by good fortune, I should become king, then her head would be crowned with mine. In short, I had an answer for everything, I agreed to anything. Would Dolores herself want me? I got her reply the next day, when I went back to the same place at the same hour; she was picking flowers again.

Then, for the first time in my life, I entered that strange and delicious state in which a woman becomes the living heart of the universe; in which her body, more precious than all the riches of Harun al-Rashid, constantly radiates more agitation than all the gold and precious stones of that great king; in which a look, a tone of voice, a laugh, a movement of the head, give incomparable happiness; in which no project surpasses in hope and anxiety that of winning her. Dolores did not speak my language, but luckily I spoke hers, with an accent and clumsily, which made her laugh or bewildered her. When she laughed, I imitated myself in order to hear her laugh again; when she did not understand me, I repeated myself patiently until the gaze cleared in the even blue of her eyes. These games, difficulties, and efforts took up so much of our already too short time, that we did not say much to each other. But what did we have to say with words? On the contrary, these difficulties became the occasion for an exquisite sport in which we leveled with each other, lost each other, caught up with each other, and in which we had nothing to win but each other, as the best of all prizes. Though far from being a chatterbox, I have never talked so much as when my tongue found itself hindered. That is another miracle that woman inspires: you talk and talk as if she were a child, as if you were becoming a child again yourself, and the only thing that counts is the reassuring sound of a voice.

Then, indeed, everything changed—Castile and the Castilians, my state of mind, and my senses. It was as if I were starting my journey again from the beginning, but this time with a favorable attitude and with curiosity, even love, for the people that was becoming my own, since it belonged to my beloved.

To give you only one example, I made myself watch again, almost beyond the limits of moderation, those bullfights that I had disdained and condemned so strongly. Instead of a bloodthirsty farce, I found a tragic fable. I must grant that, even during such a brief stay, I had time to witness so many fatal accidents, so many brave men trampled, their guts spilled out, picked up almost dead, despite speedy assistance, that I had to admit that such a spectacle, far from being a mere diversion, must be the symbol of some deeper and more ancient drama in that people's life.

Try to imagine a large crowd massed on circular steps, dressed as if for the most important holiday, at first joyous before the arrival of the bull, then suddenly silent and tense, except for shouting as if with one voice when a particularly successful pass was made. Seized by the same anguish, which obviously exceeded the event of the moment, they would finally commune, all classes mixed together, in a sort of nightmare that the entire people tirelessly played out over and over again. For that deadly and sublime game is not reserved at all for the nobles and the rich. As soon as they can walk, the children in the streets divide themselves into bulls and bullfighters and play at spilling each other's guts; for this purpose, the adults provide them with a plentiful supply of wicker horns and wooden swords. A young man cannot conquer a woman unless he has killed several bulls. Old men take constant pride in remembering how many wounds they received in this perpetual tournament. Must we not conclude that a secret tumult troubles the soul of this people for it thus endlessly to provoke death?

Soon everything seemed to me understandable, moving, and admirable. The king's somber haughtiness, the prime minister's nervousness, the restless mistrust of everyone, and each one's overeager response at any perceived threat. They explained to me why the king always wore that gold medallion containing the minute relic of a bone of an exemplary saint, bequeathed to him by his father and handed down from generation to generation. It was a way of forcefully affirming that the kings of Castile had been Christians without break or wavering since the beginning of time. The excessive violence with which Spanish males react whenever the virtue of their women is questioned is similar, as is their people's insistence on the purity of their faith: it is supposed to imply that they are descended from the most famous Christians of the Interior Sea, and of unsullied blood since the founder of that religion.

Younous tried hard to calm my brand-new fervor a little. These perpetual Christians, he explained, were until recently mostly Muslims, who only converted after the victory of the Christian armies. This apparently pure race has experienced occupation for such a long time that it is unable to distinguish between the blood that it receives from the invader and what remains of its own. The Castilians labored to lose all their memory, the better to efface their origins, which always show through. As for the virtue of their women, well, it has been put to the test so often! Far from considering such self-deception scandalous or pathetic, I saw it as the sign of great courage and vigor. In short, thanks to Dolores, I excused, understood, and loved everything about the Castilians.

The greatest difficulty still remained; as usual, it was the one for which the solution did not lie in my power. Dolores was Castilian and Christian; what was her guardian, the king of Castile, going to think about it? Would he agree to my marrying my beloved? I found out at this point how attached Pedro the Cruel was to Dolores. He had not had the good fortune to have children and treated her as his own daughter. That unhappy sovereign, whose ancestry was dubious, and for whom issue was impossible, had built himself an imaginary future and past. My idea was to take my wife with me; but what would I do if Pedro the Cruel required that his goddaughter remain in Castile? I have never confided this to anyone but you, Sire: I would have settled permanently in that court. There again, of course, I did not fail to invent justifications for myself. Since the sovereign did not have any children, Dolores would one day be his successor. Was not Providence offering me Castile as a base for winning back my own kingdom? Linked by marriage to that powerful state, my project would be greatly facilitated.

Truly, if the king had demanded it, I would have given up my birthright from my father for Dolores.

What had become of all my mistrust and severity for those who succumb in those easy combats, you will be saying. I am still unable to answer that: a speck of dust can cloud an eye, and an eyelash can make it weep. I was simply no longer the same man as the one who had landed on the coast of Spain only a few weeks earlier. I was so disturbed that I found myself thinking of Turncoat with sympathy: is betrayal for one's faith really betrayal? Are not traitors merely men enthralled by a new faith?

I no longer cared about my mission; I sought neither to elicit a reply from my hosts, nor even to ascertain the inclinations of the king and his ministers. Younous, who understood me better than anyone else in the world, was silent. I did not question him, for fear of his reply, which I didn't want to hear if it didn't suit me. I lived within my dream, as if it would last forever. I scarcely ate, I hardly slept; but does one need rest and sustenance when one is magically sustained by the fire of love? This mission, which had begun so badly, was becoming the most wonderful adventure I have ever had in a life full of travel.

In the morning, I waited for the afternoon when the court ceremonies took place, in which I might glimpse Dolores. In the afternoon, I waited for the evening, when I could talk to Dolores in the king's reception rooms. I waited all day for one of those rare, sublime moments when I might meet Dolores in the park. In public, I only caught glimpses of my love; in the salons, I only spoke to her in the presence of witnesses; in the park, we only exchanged a few fleeting words. Through naive calculation or artful innocence, Dolores allowed me to take no liberties with her. If I had had my composure, I would have hated love to be so restrained and deprived of its nature, but I needed only to see her; and she seemed fully gratified by the ardor of my eyes alone. I suffered when I saw her talking to anyone else, even the king; I cursed the freedom granted the women of that land, a freedom that nevertheless had served me well. But my excessively anxious state so visibly increased my beloved's happiness, that I was delighted by my suffering and her cruelty.

And on the day when the king finally sent me news, I was as shocked by it as if there had never been any relation between my mission and my presence in Castile, as if I had come only to win Dolores. The news was somewhat less than pleasant. Had I committed some imprudence, or had spies, planted among my servants, reported some of those free reflections that one makes when one believes oneself to be alone? Or was it that the king had finally learned of our idyll?

The fact was that I had displeased him, and they wanted me to know that. I was asked, on the sovereign's behalf, by what date I intended to terminate my stay, on the pretext that the reply I had come to seek had to be prepared. I was being informed in diplomatic terms that it was time to conclude my ambassadorial mission.

I was frantic; instead of calmly working out some guiding principle of behavior, I recklessly decided to hasten the course of my private affairs. At first, I considered carrying off my beloved. It was lucky that a few grains of common sense survived in my distraught mind. I

6. "At first I considered carrying off my beloved." Courtesy of Albert Memmi.

finally shared my thoughts with Younous, who remained silent. But this time I was in no mood to put up with his pretended reluctance: I demanded a reply.

"You will have it tomorrow," he said.

I hardly slept; in the morning I did in fact have the reply I wanted: it dawned on me clearly that I was about to commit an act of great folly. We would not have gone one league before being overtaken, then thrown in prison or executed on the spot. This was not even counting a war with Tunis, which would be a pretty outcome for an ambassador and, there again, it was assuming that Dolores would agree to follow me. The next day, I did not even speak about it again to Younous, who did not ask me anything.

Since I needed the approval of Pedro the Cruel, I abruptly sent to ask the sovereign if he would be disposed to grant me the queen's cousin as my wife. It was another act of great naivety to think that brusqueness, added to the king's dissatisfaction, would put my affairs to rights. But what else could I do? The reply came so quickly that it seemed to me they were already prepared for it. Since I was a prince and ambassador of a powerful king, Pedro the Cruel thanked me for my generosity in thinking of marrying a distant cousin of his, though he considered her his daughter. He would look on it with favor, he said. In any case, he granted me permission to become a Castilian and a Christian, in order to be a worthy husband of a Castilian, Christian woman, in accordance with the humane and religious laws of the kingdom of Castile. In conclusion, he rejoiced at these two events which, as I would certainly understand, were indissolubly linked.

Such an insolent requirement finally brought me to my senses. So, in order for me to ensure my issue, I was being required to deny myself and deny my ancestors! I immediately thanked the king in reply for the generosity with which he vouchsafed to welcome me into the bosom of the great Christian nation of Castile. I regretted, however, that I did not yet feel worthy of such an honor. Consequently, I requested permission to return to Tunis, where I would be able to report to Bologuine the results of the mission he had entrusted to me, and go into retreat to meditate on all these events. Which permission was royally given.

We left a few days later, and I never saw Dolores again. At the moment when, at the head of my men, I passed through the palace's main gate and found myself surrounded by the crowd of gapers come to watch our train, I thought I would faint from the beating of my heart; I could hardly breathe and could feel my eyes becoming moist; yes, I would have wept if I had not had so large a company and was not the focus of so many eyes. I hastened my horse's pace.

But we had hardly traveled the few leagues that separated us from the ships, than it dawned on me from what danger I had escaped. For a woman whom I hardly understood, whose worth I scarcely knew, except for her beauty (but so many bodies are as good as each other!), I had almost remained among a foreign people; I would have renounced my duty! It was true that she had paid me some attention, but had I forgotten all manly wisdom, that says that every woman wants to be fertilized and seeks protection to bring forth her fruit? Had I then no other aim than watching over just one future mother? Had I fought so hard to conquer myself that, without Dolores, I became of no consequence? Had I spent so much time finding out the exact taste of things just to find myself powerless to enjoy them alone? Oh, what a snare woman is! I felt like a man recovering from an illness, truly a terrible illness—passionate love—indeed, a kind of madness.

Now I had to consider how to account to Bologuine for the outcome of my journey. I had not even succeeded in sounding out the intentions of Pedro the Cruel. Would he accept our alliance? I had asked him. He was fearful of that dangerous honor, he had replied. What conditions would he attach to it? He could not speak of conditions when he had not reflected on the principle. Would he make an alliance with our enemies? He had not given any thought to that either. I then judged it opportune to goad him somewhat. Did he hope in the near future to undertake a war of any sort? A king never hopes to wage war, he told me firmly, but he cannot avoid it if it is imposed on him. He showed himself, in short, more cunning than I was. Probably I had been too impatient, or too disdainful of those contests, allusions, suggestions, moves back and forth, which are the delight of the ambassadors by profession. My supreme sin had been to mix my private concerns with public affairs; so that I had muddied one with the other, to no avail. But the further the ship went, the more the habitual, calming spell of the sea affected me. Soon I could not even understand how I could have forgotten the trust and interests of my friend and my king.

Soon Dolores came to resemble a phantom of my mind; a phantom that I doubted had ever belonged to this world. As for the Castilians, I would have been hard put to say what they were exactly. Since no adventure is without profit, I gained this piece of knowledge at least: peoples, like individuals, can dream; and before one passes judgment on them, one should also listen to their ravings.

The Burntfaces

After reaching Tunis, I immediately made my report to Bologuine; I told him above all how perplexed I was. My friend seemed concerned, and he had reason to be; a few weeks later, we learned through our spies that the king of Castile had promised the assistance of his fleet to the Bougians. He had, nonetheless, assured me that he had had no contact with them. Unless a king can lie, the only result of my mission had been to give Pedro the Cruel the idea of offering his support to our enemies. Bologuine did not seem incensed or even surprised. He merely drew the conclusion that he should prepare for war more quickly and make other provisions. I had less confidence and more illusions.

"And so," I exclaimed, "in our ill-fated lands, each one thinks only of attacking his neighbors."

"The explanation is easy," Bologuine said to me. "Look at the map: it's impossible for us to push north, because of the sea; impossible to go south, there is the desert, and we would have to cross it before reaching the least prey. Truly we have only one outlet, that of spreading ourselves at the expense of our neighbors to the right and left."

"But why are you so intent on extending yourselves, when you are each provided with your own kingdom?"

Bologuine looked at me in surprise, and then pursed his lips a little; that was all he allowed himself when he became annoyed.

"Come, you know that quite well."

The situation was getting serious. We could have asked for help from the kingdom of Fez, which was then governed by people who were favorable to us. We were so used to seeing the sudden seizures of power and palace revolutions, sovereigns being assassinated and replaced by their murderers, one after the other, that it was better not to trust such unstable allies.

It was then that Bologuine, with the genius of a great soldier, thought up another one of his ideas. Why not break the habitual round of alliances and misalliances? The world always expands for whoever dares to push out its limits, why not reach out to those faraway lands where the dark-skinned people called the Burntfaces live? They were said to be formidable warriors, though since they were poorly armed they easily succumbed to the white man's incursions. It would be enough to teach them our rules of combat, bolster them with a draft of trained men, and provide them with suitable arms. We would then have an inexhaustible reservoir of first-class men. Bologuine asked if I would agree to do him a great favor for the second time, by leading an ambassadorial mission to those lands.

My friend did not conceal from me that this mission would be less pleasant than the other; the journey itself would not be without danger; moreover, there was a risk that the Burntfaces would not receive us favorably. Our peoples had always treated them harshly, pillaging their women and children whenever we needed slaves. The young men, who were trained to become mercenaries, were often castrated to prevent them from leaving seed in our countries; and after they had done long service, it was not unusual for a sovereign to have them assassinated to avoid giving them large amounts in back pay. It would no doubt be hard to assuage their distrustful hostility. In short, I would run the risk of losing my life in the enterprise. But this time I felt that Bologuine was really worried; and after my behavior in Castile, I was determined to show my friend my loyalty. I consented right away.

With Younous's help, I drew up a map of our itinerary and calculated supplies and loads. For myself, I would take only a few clothes of gaudy colors and abundant ornaments, which I thought would impress the savages, and my box of precious stones that I always took with me. Taking our inspiration from the journey of the Merinid, we had a choice between two routes: following the coast as closely as possible while penetrating the hinterland just enough to find water and food, or making directly for the castle of El-Djem, an inspiring witness to what Roman power had been, and then for the Ribat of Monastir, a perfect example of the alliance of military power and faith. As Younous advised, I decided on the first solution for, as he said, one should not use up people's patience too soon. Finally, when he had helped me prepare everything, Younous asked my permission not to accompany me. It was the only time he had done this. But since it would involve returning to his native land, I put it down to some affair in which he had had a hand in the past or vestiges of pride that prevented him from returning as a slave, even a privileged one. I then remembered that he had never, since I had known him, asked to return to his native country. I agreed, despite my regret. I consoled myself by looking forward to rare discoveries and new experiences to enjoy in lands that were really foreign. I asked the king for a reduced escort, which would be more resistant in an adventure bound to be full of pitfalls, and I left immediately.

The journey actually did begin pleasantly. We left Tunis by the Ras-el-Tabia quarter, admiring its gardens and ponds as we passed. In the evening, we encamped at Kairouan, where I visited the ancient monuments, the remains of buildings erected by the Aghlabids and the Zirids, and the tombs where the saints and scholars of the law have been laid to rest. The next morning, I arose at dawn for the first time in a long while. I looked at the sky as I emerged from the tent; I breathed with the rhythm of the breeze and felt I was regaining my real pace. "What palace of stone, what ceiling of silk can give me all this?" I said to myself. Oh, I am never as happy as when I become a nomad again! I realized I was pleased at having set out, even though I had left such a friendly court. We passed by Mahdiya; then, having traversed all of the civilized country and the savannah, we finally reached the beginning of the forest. It was from then on that the journey should have become dangerous and surprising; it was neither one nor the other.

We only lost three men. The first one died of strangulation by an enormous snake, which fell on his shoulders from a tree above

7. "Our guides had told us of strange animals." Courtesy of Albert Memmi.

and coiled around him like a rope in a single movement. We cut the terrible beast with saber thrusts, but it was too late to save the poor fellow. The second man was swallowed by a crocodile before our eyes and was still screaming when all the lower part of his body was in the monster's gullet. The third one disappeared and perhaps ran away. Our guides had warned us of the existence of monstrous plants and animals, but could not show us any. We saw none of those flesh-eating flowers which, it seems, attack animals and even men with a rapidity and ferociousness forestalling any defense, nor any of those sucking lianas that enmesh the traveler and empty him slowly of his blood. We found only a heavy luxuriance everywhere, and I ended by feeling sickened by this land too well fed and bloated with water. Perhaps, despite myself, those too opulent flowers and exaggerated leaves disturbed me, as if God had made them not for us men but for some giants whose calm we were disturbing and who would spring on us to hold us to account . . . In any case, I do not like excess, whether in nature or in men, and I often sighed at the memory of our good dry earth and our plants as knotty as our people. The animals were a little less disappointing. One day we saw an enormous ox with a single horn in the middle of its forehead; another time, we saw an animal bathing whose mouth was so huge that it could have contained an entire young goat. Our amazement, however, was never so great as when we passed through an entire herd of antelopes whose necks were so long that they could graze directly on the leaves of the trees! Perhaps you do not completely believe me, Sire; as for myself, I would have doubted the truth of such stories if I had not seen all of this with my own eyes. It made me more modest; why should I doubt the testimonies of other travelers if my own can be so amazing? Unless, God forbid, I also doubt myself. But in the end, they were still only creatures of God, grazing on grass, eating fruit, or hunting living prey, which itself ate other animals; in short, what we had always been familiar with; and I realized that nature is the same everywhere.

I would also have liked to meet men somewhat different from ourselves, even if we had had to defend ourselves against them; we did not meet a single one. We sometimes sensed their furtive presence, from a few signs that our guides showed us; but they seemed to be more afraid of us than we of them. Thus, of those discoveries that I had dreamed of as I was setting out, all that remained was unsatisfied nostalgia. Our guides, who were themselves Burntfaces acclimatized to our lands, and who had made this trip several times, commented on the journey and embellished it with varied information. The more or less imaginary stories they told around the fire enthralled us more than the real marvels they vainly promised us. Balibas, who had lived with us longest, and had sharpened his wits with us, was especially adroit at adding to the interest of the lands we passed through, heightening it with anecdotes. Thus, when we entered their respective countries, he told us the stories of the land of the eunuchs and of the Grey Men.

The eunuchs, he told us, belonged to a tribe of inveterate brigands who were not content with pillaging harvests and flocks when they were hungry, which would be admissible, or with carrying off a few women when they ran short, which would be tolerable, but constantly insisted on violating the women of their sedentary neighbors, even the old women and the sick, then leaving them to the shame of their husbands, brothers, fathers, and uncles. One day, tired of waging war on them, and killing a few periodically without succeeding in discouraging the others, the sedentary folk joined together and assembled the strongest force that had ever been seen in those regions. They needed the help of many men to carry out their project. On the appointed day, they fell on the pillagers who, petrified by such numerical superiority, did not even defend themselves. The townsfolk quite calmly picked out a hundred of them, whom they carefully tied one behind the other. Then, instead of killing them, they led them off.

Nothing was heard of the captives for a few weeks until they returned to their village. They seemed strangely sad and quiet. When asked about what had happened, they obstinately refused to talk. However, it was noticed that all, without exception, thenceforth refused to share their wives' beds. That place was called the Land of the Hundred Eunuchs. It is true, Balibas added with an ambiguous smile, that the opposite is also told: it was that tribe which punished a neighboring population in that way, hence the name, which would be a title of glory rather than of wretchedness. In any case, no one again dared violate the wives of the townsfolk. But the Lord alone knows the truth.

It was the same in the case of the Grey Men: at first I thought their name was just a manner of speaking, but Balibas assured us that their skin was really that color. Since those people fed themselves exclusively on loose earth, only rarely eating the fruits and vegetables in which their country nevertheless abounds, they came to resemble what they swallowed; so that when they died, nothing remained of them but a little pile of mud, which finally dried up and dispersed as dust in the wind. There again, we did not see any of them and were obliged to believe our guides. We did see, though, that the earth of their land was grey, dull, as if petrified; even the sky seemed so strangely opaque that one had the unpleasant impression of being in a room hung with wet veils, so that one felt an irresistible urge to break through those many-layered nets and get one's head out in order not to suffocate. It is not impossible that such a landscape and such a climate might have formed such men. As for us, we were happy that nothing obliged us to linger there.

At last, we left those regions with relief—too green and humid, too lush with plants, animals, and crawling things, that prolific and insatiable nature that could easily have swallowed us—and reached savannah again, then the austere and faithful poverty of the desert. But since everything under the sun has its darker side, I had to bear with other discomforts.

Although I felt more comfortable in dry heat, that was not the case for all my men. Many of them complained of strange sensations in the back of their throats, temples, and noses. Others were possessed by an insatiable and unjustified thirst; they had to be restrained from uselessly filling their stomachs with water. Some who were really ill or anxious had nose-bleeding, which worried them extremely. They believed themselves seriously afflicted and were joyously surprised on realizing that they only had to rest for a few minutes with head thrown back in order to put an end to this terrifying episode. Even the most lighthearted, disguising their anguish in their own way in the face of these stony solitudes, grumbled about the monotony of the food and the absence of game.

What was to give me the most concern, and in fact did, was the water problem. Not knowing the country, I turned to Balibas in this respect, and he did not fail me. But shortages did occur. Our guides only let us take the exact amount of water needed—because of the weight, because of our already difficult progress, and because of their certainty of finding some water each time at a reasonable distance, since they knew the country perfectly. Once, one of these wells turned out to be dry. Our guides were not put out; there must be another one not far away, reached through a detour, which they had us make without even asking my permission; we found that one empty, too. It was only then that they came to me and suggested that we make no more halts, in order to reach the third one as soon as possible, while we could still do so. As a precaution, I forbade the men to drink all their supply, which in itself made them anxious. Luckily, the third location contained water, and everyone rushed at it without restraint. I did too, I have to confess. Oh, how fresh the water tasted, better than a woman's kiss. It was high time; we were so thirsty that our saliva was caking in our mouths, the roofs of our mouths were becoming hard, and I saw a special nervousness growing among the men, who fortunately were not aware of it. Soon nothing would have been able to calm that maddening ache. Two men disappeared on that occasion; believing that they were saving themselves, they no doubt suffered a terrible death.

We crossed another humid area and then another desert and, ten days later—that is, after a total of 103 days and 103 nights—we entered the territory of the Burntfaces; or more precisely, our guides informed us so, for at first we saw nothing. A small incident soon showed me that we had entered a different world. I had got up earlier than my companions, as I did every morning; I was about to begin my ablutions when I saw a man trying to run away; I rushed at him with my sword in my hand and shouted to alert my companions. I was about to strike the enemy down, when I noticed that it was not worth the trouble: he was a poor wretch who was carrying off some of our provisions, and still had his mouth full. Not knowing what language he might speak, I signaled to him with my hand to help himself. He looked at me with amazement and gratitude, then fell upon the food, convulsively taking as much as his arms would hold, looked at me again, then ran off without looking back, no doubt for fear that I would call him back. There was such joy in the eyes of this wretch that for a moment at least I would have given away a fortune to provoke such a response. It was then that I saw that my box of precious stones was ajar. I shouted with rage; he had deceived me by pretending that he had been looking for food! But, going closer, I saw that he had not taken anything. He really had been hungry and thirsty and to satisfy these wants, he needed biscuits and water, not stones, however beautiful they might be.

Finally, we reached the outskirts of the capital of the Burntfaces. From that point on, I took as many precautions as possible. I had already eliminated watch fires, and forbidden hunting and gathering. In addition, I ordered our weapons to be camouflaged and our caravan to be given the most peaceful appearance possible, which was in fact the case. We soon sighted a city. It was really only a village, scarcely any larger than the others but less poor, even though all the houses were still of dried mud, except for one large building, which we took to be the king's palace, or the great temple of this people. I had camp set up a few hundred yards from the first house, to show that we were not concealing ourselves and were waiting for an invitation before making our entry into the city. Then I dispatched Balibas and another guide to the king or his equivalent to test their intentions toward us. I gave them several presents for the king, his wives and, as a shot in the dark, his sorcerers. They soon came back with his answer: he had been informed of our presence in his people's lands as soon as we had crossed the frontiers; from then on, he had awaited us without hostility, otherwise we would have already been dead. That seemed to me a judicious answer, for a savage. The prince had, moreover, been very conscious of my forbidding hunting and burning wood on his land without his permission. Lastly, he authorized us to carry our arms openly. So he knew everything about us. It made me laugh at the idea of all the precautions I had taken in order not to be noticed, and I congratulated myself on having respected those people. Since all the same we were still dealing with scarcely civilized folk, I decided to wait until the following day before introducing ourselves to the king. It would be better to take the time to put our accoutrements in order and prepare our formal robes.

The Sorcerer-Prince

Our stay among the Burntfaces was both instructive and peaceful, two qualities that rarely combine. I greatly enriched my notes there and I cannot tell you, Sire, all the things I saw from which we might draw profit.

In the early days, I wondered whether I was dreaming, their customs appeared so different from ours. When our guides led us into the presence of the king and his ministers, surrounded by the people, I was greatly embarrassed, for all those people looked alike. Moreover, they wore no clothes, only a few feathers and foliage in their hair. Later on, during the holidays, which were numerous and sometimes lasted several days, it was worse, for they put over their heads and necks enormous masks, which misled us even more. It took us a long time even to distinguish the prince from his ministers and the ministers from each other. We had to resort to ruse so as not to commit an error that would be a breach of etiquette and insult the hierarchy. In fact, it was quite simple: the most important had the right to the highest and most abundant foliage. That amused us and at first we thought we were justified in despising those savages; then I remembered that the Castilians, who thought they were the most civilized people on earth, hardly behaved any differently, since they made themselves taller with hats, combs, and heels. And don't we ourselves reserve the largest and most valuable turbans for the highest officials? With the savages, it was feathers and greenery; the main thing, everywhere, is to exceed everyone else in height.

Moreover, we had been warned that they were exceedingly wretched. What makes a man or a people wretched? After living with the Burntfaces, inhabiting their huts and eating their food, I no longer know how to answer. I have seen men who are as happy as we can be—when we are—and as proud. They had thick lips and large flattened noses, but they thought they were all handsome and therefore constantly paid each other compliments. They called each other "Beautiful Hunter," "Beautiful Fisherman," "Beautiful Horseman"; one of them, who really was extremely ugly, had himself called "Beautiful Ugly Man"! Since they thought themselves beautiful and treated each other as such, wasn't that enough to satisfy anyone? They were of an indistinguishable blackness; but they recognized each other, and it was us, the whites, who seemed dislocated and, feeling confused, huddled together nervously in a bunch. They were naked, they were poor; in their ceremonies, it was all done with plants, leaves, and branches. But those fragile constructions were supposed to represent sumptuous palaces, magnificent temples, and triumphal arches. Those officiating, seated on those ephemeral thrones and adorned with those pathetic crowns, bestrode wondrous impatient beasts, and led forth countless armies to fabulous victories.

The last point intrigued me, though: where had they heard all that? For hundreds of leagues around there were neither temples nor palaces, nor any building of any size, except those poor huts, the largest of which could hardly match our smallest buildings. I shared my doubts with Balibas. In order to invent this splendid past, hadn't his people borrowed a little from travelers' tales? The guide almost lost his temper. He showed me old coins that the Burntfaces no longer used, but piously preserved in memory of their age of greatness, and a few objects, the meaning of which he could not tell me. No, no; to be sure his people had really held sovereignty in far-off times over immense regions, prodigiously fertile lands, and cities overflowing with wealth. I did not dare respond to the good Balibas that I had the feeling that I recognized Rumi coins, of which there are so many in our land; and that the objects were none other than fragments of household utensils that one can buy in our souks. From malice, though, I could not prevent myself from asking him where those marvelous lands that his people had formerly conquered were. Balibas answered me with childish stories about supposed cataclysms engulfing multitudes of peoples and entire civilizations. For good measure, he added talking animals and heroes who by means of metamorphoses, could sail in midair or in the depths of the oceans. In short, I never could work out whether his people was raving, inventing a rich history, or if it preserved some distorted memory of a real past.

I congratulated myself on belonging to such a rational people, whose wise men are so worthy of respect and whose tradition, always reliable, contains no fantastic tales. But, in the last analysis, though some peoples may be richer in gold or grain, no people is really without heritage, thanks to its imagination. And since at heart men are everywhere alike, any man, even a thousand leagues from our cities and sophisticated courts, can teach us something about ourselves.

My tablets, in any case, were greatly enriched there. I asked as many questions as I could without being indiscreet. I am not sure whether I always understood the replies, especially in the beginning when I did not yet speak the language of the Burntfaces. I often tried to describe some rite that fascinated me through its originality, or to sketch an object whose form pleased me, without penetrating the purpose of either. On other occasions, I came across some useful suggestion I might use in the future. For example, like any other prince, the king of the Burntfaces had his own musicians. I noticed the presence of a large cat among them, the tail of which was pulled without fail before they began a piece. When I asked about it, they explained what was expected of the poor creature. The king's musicians, people sensitive both as artists and as court employees, frequently disagreed when they were tuning their instruments, particularly their form of viola, of which I have brought back several sketches and a miniature in carved wood. They rarely succeeded in choosing the same tone initially. They therefore decided to turn to a cat, whose meows they provoked and from which everyone could tune himself without feeling diminished. That at least is what I think I understood from their excited explanations.

However, I had not made such a long journey for the sake of enriching my notes. I waited with patience and some anxiousness for the negotiations to begin. They began with an ease that was disconcerting. I had been ready for lengthy, delicate maneuvers, in which I would have to use my wits in order to convince these people of our disinterestedness and the profit that would accrue entirely on their side from our bargain. They did not give me time enough. After I had stated the matter to the council assembled around the king, and they had heard me out in complete silence, they paid so little attention to me and my companions that we finally went off for walks while awaiting the conclusion of their endless parlaying. Their procedure was simple: each one talked in turn until he was exhausted, and they went on like that as long as necessary. It lasted three days, during which all the advantages and disadvantages of my proposition for them were carefully weighed.

Only one thing disturbed them—why was it that my king and master had sent me so far away, why had I accepted such a dangerous adventure, if my own people would only gain slight benefit from it? They not only did not find it shocking or suspect that we were pursuing our own interests in coming to them but also, they added frankly, the more our motives were based on self-interest, the more weight they would give them. I had to change my strategy quickly; I explained emotionally how we were constrained to make war in order to protect ourselves against fearful enemies. They seemed very satisfied with that. Finally, the council, having clearly ascertained where its people's interest and ours lay, gave me its agreement through the king.

Our difficulties did not stop there. Bologuine was hoping for an initial contingent of ten thousand men, followed by some others at regular intervals. I reluctantly observed that they would not be able to supply us with those: illness, famine, and raids periodically decimated them. Of course, I offered them gold as payment. They found that very funny: I then learned that they had gold or could get it in plenty if they took the trouble to look, though we could not get them to tell us where. No, they wanted what they did not possess, and valued most: supplies for feeding and defending themselves. I accepted hastily, for the exchange would be less costly for us. We finally agreed that they would provide us with an annual contingent of three thousand men, in return for grain, salt, and arms.

One last misunderstanding, the greatest one, occurred when we were about to seal our agreement, and another council meeting, although less lengthy than the preceding one, had to be held: I had noticed, fortunately in time, that the king was proposing to send us three thousand old men. I thought he was trying to cheat us, but he gave me so many arguments in favor of his decisions, that I clearly saw he had the best of intentions. The Burntfaces themselves needed all their able-bodied boys for farming and hunting; that is why they were offering their old men to me. Despite this, our interests would not suffer: old men, he told me, are craftier and more responsible, which is essential in the art of war; moreover, it was better to avoid engaging young men, especially foreigners, since they would have little self-control and risked, through unheeding hotheadedness and excess energy, falling into needless killing, which would make the return of peace more difficult. I found those arguments quite amazing, though not devoid of sense. It was difficult for me to explain that for our wars young men were the most suitable since we did not systematically avoid killing our adversaries, whom we hated profoundly, and that moreover our enemies also used combatants of the same age. He parried that all we need do was ask them also to put only old men on the line. "They will never agree," I said, "for they too want to kill us." Moreover, since we were at war, we did not speak to each other anymore. He found all of that quite stupid, for the purpose of war is not to destroy the lives and goods of one's adversary, but to increase one's own. And how can peace be reestablished if one does not maintain contact with the enemy? I could only admit that he was right; but I could not change my people's customs and we both had to accept it. I increased the quantity of arms and grain, and after consulting with the council, he agreed to this new arrangement.

We organized the annual relay of our future hired soldiers: each year, three thousand men would join our army's ranks. This mercenary contingent, which would therefore consist of nine thousand men in three years, would have to do six years of service, distributed as follows: two years of training, two years of fighting, and two years of defense. At the end of the first six years, three thousand of them would be free to go home, on condition that they be immediately replaced by an equivalent contingent; so that we would always have nine thousand Burntfaces available and our suppliers could regulate returns on the basis of their ability to supply men to replace them. Of course, we would pay again for each new conscript. The king had not realized that his young men might decide not to return and we would then not have to pay anything more. I am ashamed to say that I refrained from pointing this out to him. But is it an ambassador's role to be fair to both his hosts and his own country? Yet again, I admired Bologuine's genius, which procured for us with negotiation what he could not get with force.

In any case, the king of the Burntfaces seemed happy with our arrangement. I was anxious to find out what his people would think of it, but as soon as the agreement was made known, he gave an enthusiastic party for us without any circumspection at all. I wondered why people protest so strongly when their brothers are carried off, while they themselves give them up so easily for a little gold. I thought that at least the parents of our future conscripts would not exactly applaud a barter that deprived them of their children. It was explained to me that the Burntfaces had complete confidence in the wisdom of their princes, who were incapable of acting against their interests. The reason is this: the prince, whose real title was Sorcerer-Prince, not only held the rights of life and death over his subjects, but also controlled the elements of nature. It was he who made the plants grow and ensured the fertility of women, fended off illness and healed livestock, tempered the heat and calmed the winds. It would be impossible to list all his powers; in sum, he could bring about whatever his people needed. Hiding our disbelief for the moment, in order not to offend our hosts, we asked them whether he ever failed in what he undertook. With all simplicity, they answered that he did. Although the sorcerer-prince was all-powerful over living things and the elements, he also made it a point of honor to be supreme in wisdom; if, despite the prince's efforts, a catastrophe was impossible to prevent, they sacrificed the best they had: that is, the prince himself, who agreed to this with all his heart. And everyone accompanied him weeping to the stake. We could not hide our surprise at this solution. A serious young man in my retinue, just starting out in diplomacy, wanted to explain to our friends the savages that by that they lost their prince without avoiding misfortune. I would not let him. Besides the fact that it is never appropriate to criticize one's hosts, it is useless to try to protect a people against itself. If it loves itself, it will certainly find what it needs; if it hates itself, it will be its own worst enemy; and if it lets itself die, nothing can save it from its death.

We finally sealed our agreement. Toward that end, the king suggested to me that we mix bloods and exchange wives; in that way, Balibas told me, we would become brothers forever. That is one of the most astounding habits of these savages. As soon as they have agreed on a favorable barter or conquered an enemy people, instead of pressing their advantage, cheating, and trying to get the most, they offer gifts and are so polite to their former enemy that they oblige him to become their ally. Once their interests are intimately linked, no one has any advantage any more in damaging the other.

And so I gave some of my blood; but since I had not brought any women, all I could do was promise some, in the hope that time would lead them to forget this sensitive clause, which is little practiced among us.

Then we entered upon a new, lengthy period of rejoicing, with processions, dances, disguises, and games of all sorts. This led us to conclude that among the Burntfaces the total number of holidays exceeded that of working days, which raised our envy. I dispatched a message to Bologuine to inform him of the results of my mission. I expressed pleasure at our success, modestly adding that this time we were dealing with simple folk, lacking in all those qualities that in our parts have led political genius to reach such heights.

Bologuine's Death

While we were making preparations to undertake the exceedingly long journey again, the sorcerer-prince made me an unexpected proposal: he had been so satisfied with my diplomatic talents that he offered to make me his personal counselor. It was a great honor since that was the title of his prime minister. With much surprise, I refused at first; I reminded him that I already had a master who, moreover, was my friend. In addition, I had my own mission: I wanted to win back my lost kingdom. That made him laugh; among the Burntfaces, reigning was a fearful duty that no one would think of pursuing. As for my present master, he would take care of him. In short, he refused to give up and took it on himself to send another messenger to Bologuine right away asking him to relinquish me for an additional number of troops.

I let him proceed for, on reflection, it did not displease me. I felt comfortable with the savages, and so did my companions; we lived free from care in agreeable and continually renewed amazement; isn't that how our sages describe Paradise? As soon as that Eden palled, nothing would stop me from leaving it. Moreover, when one has a little wisdom, one should be able to live anywhere. Lastly, why should I not confess this: it was the first time that anyone had offered me the seat at the king's right hand. Even with Bologuine, I had been mostly the old companion in arms and confidant: my friend gave me hardly any chance to share in the responsibility for official business. Perhaps I would only be the prime minister of a sorcerer-prince, but I could never have been as close to power as among these savages, and short of being king, once in my life at least I would have held the foremost position. Also, wasn't this in the interest of Bologuine? From down there, I could oversee our exchange all the better. While waiting for the courier's return, I began to exercise my functions, on an interim basis at least.

One piece of information that I had chanced to hear made me uneasy, however. I had asked whom I was succeeding. "Nobody," they told me; the position had been vacant for several months and no one wanted it. I expressed surprise. It was because most of the private counselors came to a bad end, I was told; however dedicated and subtle they are, after a few years, or even a few months, they fall into disfavor and pay with their lives, or at least with exile, for their unpopularity. I then remembered that the prince himself was sometimes put to death; what would happen to his prime minister then? I was told that naturally he was sacrificed at the same time as his master.

All of that displeased me highly; but, I told myself again, one always pays dearly for power; and if my master, the prince, paid with his life, how could I bargain for mine? He who goes in front gets the first knocks. As for falling into disfavor, I was a seasoned enough diplomat not to commit the mistakes of my predecessors; I had learned the hard way so many times that you can lose through your character what you have won by cleverness and hard work. Those unfortunate fellows had believed, I assume, that they had to tell the king everything. I decided to tell the sorcerer-prince and his people only what they liked to hear. That is the great secret of all political behavior: you have to know how to keep quiet. In short, I found still more arguments to suit my wishes.

Sometime later, when Bologuine was generous enough to inform me that, while sorry to lose me, he was setting me free, I gave my definite agreement to the sorcerer-prince. The most difficult thing left was to take off my clothes and dress like the Burntfaces—that is, in only a few feathers stuck into foliage. It is true, though, that I had more than anyone else, except the king.

My functions consisted essentially of walking among the people for half of the day and telling the prince about it during the other half. This use of time seemed to me very judicious and I resolved to establish it later in my own kingdom. For whom does one reign, if not for the people? And in order to find out people's needs, isn't it best to listen to them? It was during one of these walks that I had the pleasure of discovering an old man who had known Younous. He told me Younous's sad story. His intelligence having been admired from his youth, he had had a late-born son, whom he had resolved to bring up to resemble himself, when the son was carried away in a raid. He never found any trace of him. In order to avoid suffering such pain over again, he never again touched a woman and never returned to his country. I thought I understood why he had become so attached to me. Would to Heaven that I should not disappoint him also! I swore to myself with emotion that I would try to be a worthy son of Younous. I questioned the old man further to find out what else Younous was—a great personage, an ordinary man, or a poor one. My informant answered me in a strangely evasive way, and I could find out nothing else, despite my insistence.

It was when everything seemed to be succeeding for me again that once again everything collapsed. One afternoon, when I was trying to slumber despite the infernal heat, the terrible news arrived that Bologuine had died. Oh, however brightly they may burn, all firebrands are destined for ashes!

My sorrow wrung my heart and I could not hold back my laments. Bologuine had been killed! My own brother had been killed! My other self, better than I was, for he had the strength of his passion and the courage of his severity! Oh, Bologuine, the most royal prince I have ever known! He who had won the throne purely through his own virtue! Violent and cruel he was sometimes, but one has to accept that; only the joining of extreme emotions in the service of a single idea makes true leaders and princes. And if I have turned out to be less glorious, it is because I have not desired anything with sufficient violence—neither power, nor virtue, nor pleasure. It was after I experienced this sorrow that this now familiar beast in my chest first made itself felt.

I gained a few details about the circumstances of my friend's death. He had left Tunis once again to punish some rebels who kept disrupting order in the kingdom. Bologuine always reacted promptly to such disturbances: "If there is no order there is no law, and if there is no law there is no kingdom," he used to say. However, fatigued by so many expeditions, or by then trusting too much in his prestige alone, for once he showed clemency. As he returned, he had the imprudence, too, a rare thing with him, to be alone with only a few guards: he and his small band were massacred, by those very people to whom he had shown mercy. Thus his very death proved how right his way of living was. As if Providence itself had ceased to help Bologuine, a few days later D'hou's body was found riddled with lance wounds. But he himself was surrounded by corpses: the young scoffer had died like a prince, with his sword in his hand. Yes, like a prince, the son of a prince! What a mystery divine will is, striking down the best of us like that!

Relieved that the man who had harassed them so much had died, the people of Bougie behaved in an unworthy manner. They bought his corpse from his murderers for a price in gold, profaned it in a thousand ways, then, to complete the disgrace, cut off his male organ and put it in his mouth. Finally, tired of amusing themselves with it, they cut off his head, which was beginning to go bad, and sent it to the Tunisians so that the people could see with their own eyes what remained of their king. Confronted with the death of their illustrious king martyred in such a terrible way, the Tunisians reacted unexpectedly: they made him a saint.

They made a saint of him, and then quickly forgot him. It was easy to forget him, since the new king was more tolerant than Bologuine: soon they were allowed to drink, sing, and dance again. From time to time someone reminisced aloud about the virtuous age of Bologuine, then they murmured with a sigh that he had forbidden some quite innocent pleasures—or even that his taste for greatness had made him forget the simple happiness of his subjects.

I myself lost everything, in one fell swoop. I would no longer have the help of his experience in winning back my kingdom. Having trusted too much in Bologuine's friendship to think of building up some private resources, I found myself as destitute as a beggar. My political glory rested on his, and had grown with his career; this was borne home to me immediately. When this terrible news arrived, our mission became meaningless. I was no longer the prestigious leader of a proud mission. With our sumptuous clothes and over-opulent accoutrements, we resembled rather some rich puppets, who had long been suspended from Bologuine's distant power and whose strings had just been cut. Our very riches became dangerously tempting for the impoverished masses; we read it in the eyes of the Burntfaces who a moment before had been respectful and now were covetous and already hostile. Such is the secret law: feared, we were valued and admirable friends; vulnerable, we became prey. Remembering how naively they defended their interests, I also feared their anger at the annulment of our bargain. I did not even think that the savages' behavior was deceptive: they were like all human beings.

I assembled my companions and outlined the situation; they agreed we should leave as quickly as possible. The most difficult thing would be doing without porters. I asked them all to abandon most of their personal effects and, what pained them the most, the gifts they had received. To set an example, I gave up, surprisingly without regret, my coffer of precious stones, which on the journey out had occupied an entire porter. I thought it would be imprudent to announce our departure, even to Balibas. On the contrary, I asked permission to prolong our stay in order to put our things in better order. The next day, under the pretext of distracting ourselves from our sorrow by hunting, I took out all my men and, pushing our horses to their utmost, we hastily distanced ourselves from the capital of the Burntfaces. Soon we crossed the frontier, and I was glad to be able to dress like my companions again, which was essential for winning back their respect.

Once again, there was no question of returning to Tunis, which had likely been overrun by the people of Bougia or their allies. Fortunately, I heard along the way that Fez was still in the hands of people not on our enemies' side, and so I made for it. I arrived at the beginning of the New Year and in time for the holidays that usher it in. I was welcomed there, and had the joy of finding Younous, who had correctly thought I would head for that friendly city. I saw clearly that my friend was wise. Fez was no longer the sumptuous city of yore. Many people had been slain there; so much blood can never be replaced. The population had become sparser, its vitality sapped; many of its shining lights had moved away, so that its diminished substance seemed reduced to a few scattered monuments, the illustrious witnesses to a past splendor. But where could I go? I was tired of having to constantly change port. I was also tired of seeking my fortune in the world of politics, where I always had to measure my steps, discover where the trap was hidden, and where the real power lay, so I might usefully throw in my lot.

I was thinking of retiring to the desert when, out of the blue, a new arrangement came up. You'll see for yourself, I did not really know why I responded. Perhaps I was in such despair I would have accepted anything; or, on the contrary, perhaps I was not as weary and surfeited with adventures as I had thought and, despite myself, I obstinately hoped something new would result from the incessant agitation that makes up a lifetime.

In the first place, I decided to go and pay respects to my friend's tomb. Bologuine was buried at the Tunisian frontier, in a little village that had not existed in his lifetime but was founded and had grown up around the memory of the great deceased leader. The spot gradually became a place of pilgrimage. The inhabitants of the region clustered there to serve travelers' needs so that, through an ironic twist of fate, his assassins were the founders of the only town perpetuating Bologuine's memory. It is even said that the custodians of the mausoleum were originally chosen from those who had wounded him the first and had claimed this macabre privilege. Their sons, quickly forgetting who they had been, and believing themselves to be the most faithful and surest defenders of Bologuine's memory, began to hate his enemies, the people of Bougia, from whom in fact they were descended.

In the same way, the Castilians thought they were pure Castilians, though they descended from the Moorish invaders. Bologuine's assassins believed themselves dyed-in-the-wool Tunisians, though they were conquerors from Bougia, for a long time the implacable enemies of Tunis. And no doubt the first had become Castilians rather than Moors, and the second Tunisians rather than Bougians, because they really believed that was what they were. But, oh Lord, is it right that we bear witness to our respective heavens and religions so loudly, and cut each other's throats in their names, when no one is sure of his ancestors? And when some of those we kill may be our own brothers and cousins?

Al-Kahin

Like any other edifice held up by a single pillar, Bologuine's labor collapsed all at once. When they gained control of the kingdom, the Bougians massacred all the supporters of the dead sovereign. In their enthusiasm, they even punished tribes that had accepted Bologuine's yoke only unwillingly. Revolt broke out in the land; the nomads began their raids again, the mountain-dwellers murdered the representatives of authority, the villagers cut the roads leading to their groves. The neighbors, who had long shown respect, began gnawing away at the frontiers, just like jackals that only attack the dying. Anarchy reigned in that wretched land, ungoverned once again. When I remembered my friend's unjust death, I indulged in a certain satisfaction and, despite the people's misfortune, I ardently wished to contribute to the troubles besetting Bougia.

It was then that the last Zenata revolt broke out, under a new leader. Those mountain peasants never wearied of rebelling. When a people wants to secede, it is usually because it is rich and wishes to keep its goods for itself; when one people wants to dominate another, it is because it covets its riches. The Zenata were poor, but which of us was more insane—the Zenata who had been fighting for centuries for a freedom that would not make a jot of difference to their absolute impoverishment, or their powerful neighbors, bent on pursuing a wretched prey that had nothing to offer them but its poverty? One day, this reciprocal madness came to an end; let me tell you, Sire, the price that was paid for this belated return to sanity. In any case, once again, a new captain arose—that is, a leader who was more daring or more skillful than the others were, and war started up again.

8. "Al-Kahin." Courtesy of Albert Memmi.

I decided to join the rebels. This surprised some, since the Zenata had given Bologuine much trouble, and I had even on occasion fought against them on my friend's behalf. How could I offer my sword to those who the day before had been our enemies? Nevertheless, I had several good reasons. I wanted to avenge Bologuine; what better way than joining the enemies of his murderers, even if they had formerly been his own enemies? I thought I might at the same time reap some personal advantage: after the victory, surely my new allies would in gratitude give me their support. Lastly, I believed—perhaps somewhat naively—that the right cause always finds the right solution. In short, by joining in the struggle of this rebellious people, I was acting for the best, honoring Bologuine's memory, and cultivating my own interests . . . That is how I reasoned, at least, for perhaps all those reasons were false and the only real one was that at the time I didn't know what to do with myself. Be that as it may, I summoned the remainder of my followers and went to meet the new chief of the Zenatas, whose name they had told me was al-Kahin.

I have seldom come in contact with a warrior who enjoyed warring so much, who was so made for fighting. Recklessly daring in battle, transporting himself into the most critical situations (instead of sparing himself as so many leaders do, under the pretext that their lives are too valuable), requiring for himself the same hardships as his most humble soldiers, in a way he forced fate to respond to his dedication with a deserved triumph. When he won a victory, he pursued the routed army, exterminating it with such energy that we were shocked, but could not prevent ourselves from admiring him. When he celebrated some lofty deed, he did it with excessive, almost indecent joy, but a joy we eventually understood and shared, it had so much vivacity in it. When things went against him, he was no less surprising; he became so furious that he began insulting both fortune and men, reaching the extremes of blasphemy; or, livid and silent, he refused all food, and was capable of rash deeds that were dangerous even for his intimates.

All that, which could have been repulsive, was in him sublime: he seemed so convinced of his virtue, which was real, and of the justice of his cause, which was just as real. He was also said to be a soothsayer, because of the numerous dreams he had, the meaning of which he followed carefully. To round out his portrait for you, I should recall his insolent good looks—flaming red hair, green eyes, and the elegance of a large, beautiful animal, noble and supple in the smallest movement of the head or hand, inspiring you with enthusiasm whether you liked it or not. He was, in sum, one of those men whose very departures from accepted norms are never merely vulgar, but at the same time audacious and attractive, leading you naturally into acts of madness, success, and greatness.

From the first moment, you see, I was won over and let him see this. It was hard for me, though, to convince him of my loyalty. He had not forgotten I had formerly belonged to the one he detested as the oppressor of his people. Remembering the lesson of the Burntfaces, I left aside the arguments based on morality, the nobility of his enterprise and why I desired to contribute to it, and said to him abruptly:

"Man is made in such a way that he talks only of virtue and acts only in his own interests. Here are my interests: I want revenge for Bologuine; and if I serve you well, I hope you will help me in turn, when victory has been won." Pleasantly surprised for once, al-Kahin gave me his agreement and even his respect, which was not misplaced.

Among those close to my new leader, I had the unpleasant surprise of finding Tacpharinas, the poet I had had sent away from the court of Fez, when I was chief secretary, because he had accused Turncoat of treachery. His function now was to compose songs for the army, and more importantly to interpret al-Kahin's dreams, which made him one of the few counselors to whom our leader sometimes listened. I was regretfully considering leaving the field to him, when Tacpharinas came himself and asked me to forget our differences, for the good of our common cause. I accepted immediately, all the more gratefully since I owed him my apologies. I told him he had been right about Turncoat, who had in fact plotted against Bologuine. What I had taken as spite was merely clear-sightedness. I regretted having given in to the harsh calculations of Turncoat, who wanted to eliminate an embarrassing witness. Tacpharinas responded by telling me that he had ceased to view me as an ambitious man when he had heard of my limitless devotion to Bologuine; since then he had regretted having done me harm.

I asked him out of curiosity how he had known about Turncoat's treachery.

"No one told me," he said. "I guessed it; Turncoat couldn't be anything but a traitor; he was an actor, he needed many roles to play."

I even ventured to ask him about the somber look he always wore and had made me dislike him because I thought it was partly feigned.

"Don't have any illusions," he answered, "The true poet cannot be cheerful; he knows man's sorrow too well, and his imagination does not leave him in peace. Look, even here, you see all our fiery, eager comrades; how many of them will still be alive in a few weeks' time? I cannot help imagining them wounded, with their limbs or faces torn off, bleeding, screaming with pain, or abandoned and gasping their last on the battlefield."

"Then why do you lend your hand to such ventures?" I said.

"Because these men are my brothers and their sufferings are my own." In short, he changed my mind about poets; we were so pleased with each other that we embraced and swore mutual fidelity. From then on my friendship with him was such that I couldn't understand any longer how I could have hated him.

At first, our affairs went as well as they could possibly have. Motivated by the twofold incentive of the holiness of their cause and their hatred for the enemy, fused in their love of liberty, our men did wonders. In an impressive ride we surged down from the mountains, crushing on our way all the positions that the Bougians had hastily set up. We rushed to the assault, shouting with all our hearts, thirsty for vengeance: "You bastardly son of a dog and a hyena, I'm going to eat your liver! I'm going to drink from your skull!" From time to time it did happen that a warrior, drunk with combat, or wanting to show his disdain, would drink a few drops of enemy blood, which he spat out immediately. The women introduced such excess, such determination for vengeance, that it increased our amazement at those unfathomable creatures. Those who in a previous battle had lost a father, husband, or brother, tore out the vanquished's liver and actually began chewing until, sickened by it, they vomited. Others fell upon the corpses until there was nothing human left in them, until their faces were no longer faces and their mouths no longer mouths. Some of them made bloody necklaces with the noses and ears of defeated enemies. This is the fate of oppressors when they fall into the hands of their victims.

The day after these victories, whether large or small, we celebrated: in other words, we ate, but mostly drank, until we disgorged;

we shouted instead of singing, for it is very natural for man to shout and become a beast again as soon as he loses control of his reason; we flung ourselves on the women—who at first enjoyed it but then became more and more terrified—obliging them to accept the male seed, as the earth must accept drunkards' vomit. Despite my deep devotion to my friends' cause, I did not enjoy those moments at all. Sadness overcame me; it made me foreign to what surrounded me, making me wonder why I was there, and even why I wanted so much to be king. Since I'm used to doing without superfluous things and sometimes even those that are necessary, fearing neither fatigue, nor heat, nor cold, abundance really makes no difference to me. What about women? The pleasure they give is great, but when one wants it one woman is as good as another; as for what comes after, one cannot rely on a person for whom one feels sorry. Regarding the power one has over them, perhaps I don't have such respect for my fellows that I could get much pleasure from dominating them. Then why else? In order to preserve my father's heritage and pass it on to a son? I have not known the former, and probably shan't know the latter either.

The morning would happily dispel these debilitating thoughts. The men, who had fallen asleep in the midst of their own leavings, recovered their dignity again; the women, who had washed and arranged themselves, bearing no grudges, enthusiastically prepared the food for the camp; and I, like everyone else, got ready to continue the unending fight, both my own struggle and the one I shared with my comrades.

We crossed the whole plain as far as the coast; and I found the sea again! Oh, besides the desert, only the sea gives me that feeling of immense freedom! After the mountain paths, where the foot must test its hold before stepping and the eye is the prisoner of the faltering foot, suddenly the universe opens up limitlessly, and for a long while one can hardly believe one's deliverance. I daydreamed hour after hour, crouching down by the water to watch the light ceaselessly changing, letting the powerful rhythm of the swell invade me. In the meantime (what an irony this was!), behind me, while I contemplated this fathomless spectacle of eternity, the instruments of death were feverishly being readied. Arms were being sharpened on whetstones, harness looked over, animals groomed, and a new supply of biscuits hastily baked. High spirits such as I have never seen in a regular army held sway; those of a people under arms. A changed man, Tacpharinas went back and forth across the camp, teaching and listening to couplets composed by himself or some wandering poet, so that through his efforts, multiplied by the common ardor, everyone shared in an intoxicating, sacred game. Even women and children contributed to the collective enthusiasm, singing war marches and hymns to victory—in other words, to the enemy's defeat and destruction. It was one of al-Kahin's ideas that the warriors should always have before their eyes, exposed to the same dangers, those for whom they are fighting, who would have their throats cut or be sold as slaves if the combatants gave up. I myself kept among my followers a blonde Circassian woman, with golden hair and green tigress's eyes, and with whom I had acquired the habit of regular relations; a most beautiful creature, less affectionate than faithful and reliable, the desert virtues that I appreciated the most. Moreover, she did not speak my language and I did not speak hers, which was a great advantage; I did not understand her complaints, which prevented me from being annoyed by them; she could insult me without my being irritated. Likewise, the affection of horses is only as precious as it is because they do not talk. It was enough for me to wonder each night and day at her being such a woman, at her having received from the Creator such a handsome croup, and breasts that she carried with admirable naturalness and confidence. My tent seemed empty when I did not find her there, and I found myself feeling that I too had someone to defend. I despised this concern, but it would not go away so easily. The human female is a pleasant snare that takes us back to our childhood and, despite myself, I was beginning to feel the effects of age, which also took me back to the weaknesses of a child. In short, I was more attached to her than I had ever allowed myself to be before; more perhaps than to Dolores, with whom I had not had carnal relations.

Since we had reached the shore, we had had fewer occasions for doing battle; we missed them and it was threatening to soften us. The stops were longer and sometimes more durable constructions were built, as if in the depths of his heart man's only desire is to settle down. I myself took advantage of the leisure and that great assembly of diverse peoples to remark on a multitude of new customs, objects, arms, and tools, even recipes and games, that I thought would enrich my people later. Al-Kahin restricted himself to sending many swift raids into the interior. But the exaltation that had plucked us from the mountains and thrust us across the lowlands had infected the people there. The Zenata chief cleverly sent them emissaries announcing our arrival as liberators, not as conquerors. The peasants, fortified by the mere sight of our vanguard, attacked the Bougian garrisons themselves and annihilated them without waiting for us. Then they received us as brothers and all we had to do was rejoice together. Soon, besides the support of the mountain people and the farmers of the plain, we received that of the coastal peoples. Thanks to the boats that the fishermen made available to us, we even had the rudiments of a fleet. Something that had been intended as an uprising was changing into the beginnings of an empire, of which al-Kahin was the hero and we his companions in the dawning legend.

At least, that was what we hoped, for at the same time the Bougians were pulling themselves together. They changed their general and reformed their army, which had abandoned itself to the ease of the capital and the gentleness of the conquered lands. Slowly but surely, we felt the difference between the discipline and efficiency of a regular army and the hot-blooded but disorderly enthusiasm of our irregulars. Our patrols, which had always returned victorious and loaded with booty taken from a cowering enemy, frequently no longer came back, having been decimated or taken prisoner. The few who escaped told with terror of the fearful tortures practiced by the Bougians. Thenceforth, they were heard out in troubled silence.

We knew we could not win in large, pitched battles; if we were losing in guerrilla fights, our situation was becoming dangerous. We ourselves had to think of a change in tactics. Fortunately, weighed down and too far from their bases, the Bougians could not maintain themselves for long on a war footing; they needed quick victories. War is one of those games in which, in order to win, one has only to wait for the adversary to make mistakes; we had to play for time, in order to wear out and discourage our enemy. But knowing how to wait was a strength that al-Kahin lacked. He began tiring of an enterprise that was dragging on and no longer demanded his virtues of boldness and daring. Besides, we could not reasonably hope to hold all the country that we had occupied so rapidly. At the insistence of the council and Tacpharinas, al-Kahin decided to send an ambassador to Damascus, to suggest that he and the vizier make a bargain: in exchange for the protection of Damascus, of which state we would become vassals, we would keep only the Zenata territory, slightly enlarged; the remainder we would offer to the vizier, if he would agree to become our strong ally. The Bougians would have received their punishment in any case, and we only really wanted to remain free in the mountains.

There again, we had to wait for the result of the negotiations and our emissary's return. This was too much for al-Kahin, whose impatience was leading him into imprudent acts more and more often. Sometimes he raised the siege too early from around an enemy garrison that, taken by surprise and despairing, was only waiting for the deathblow; at other times, he hastily pursued an adversary who was too powerful, on whose foolishness or terror he had been banking. It is true that he was a lucky player, repeatedly attacking, and his victories were more than his failures. But it was becoming obvious that al-Kahin's qualities themselves, that had served us so well, were now threatening to lead us to ruin.

Our leader had too close a knowledge of warfare not to sense this as well as we did. But rather than changing his ways, he grew angry at fortune, which had turned against him, his men whom he accused of softening up, and us, his lieutenants, whose anxiety he despised. He began drinking from morning on. Luckily, it was not noticeable in the camp because of the distinction in his bearing and the concise way he talked, always quite flawless; but he would become brutal and often disconcertingly vicious, in the most dangerous way, silently as a camel does. The men sensed their captain's state of mind and the seriousness of the situation came home to them. Their mood of lighthearted cheer darkened and, without wanting to, they sought imaginary food for their anxiety. Before we had caught a glimpse of the Bougian advance troops, alarming rumors were circulating in our ranks about new arms that our enemies had invented, or the size of their army, that surely through sheer numbers would thrust us into the sea.

No one dared voice to al-Kahin the only reasonable solution: we should no longer seek to engage the Bougians, who were too powerful for us. We should fall back on our main bases: thenceforth, we would only be safe in the hills. At last, in the face of imminent danger, Tacpharinas said aloud in the council what we were all thinking. We were continually more obliged to cluster in the peninsula where we were encamped: sooner or later, the Bougians would block the entry.

"We must flee as fast as possible," Tacpharinas concluded, addressing al-Kahin, "And may God grant that we manage to escape the trap in which our enemies want to shut us!"

At the very idea of retreating, and at the agonizing accuracy of this reasoning, al-Kahin went into a rage, losing all control of himself. He drew his sword, threw himself at Tacpharinas, and killed him.

"Up to now," he shouted at the poet breathing his last, "All you have done is tell me to stop; now you are pushing me to run, but it's only to run away!"

If it had not been for the dangers of the situation, our captain's glorious past, and the fact that he was obviously the worse for drink, I would have abandoned everything on the spot. Oh, how light and playful the evening drunkenness can be, while how silent and murderous is that of the morning!

The next day, al-Kahin told us his decision: scorning our opinion, instead of withdrawing, he was going to the attack again. It had always worked for him, and he refused to change his methods—moreover, he had received confirmation of this course in a dream. He told us that he had already drawn up a new plan. He had asked the fishing people who supported us to bring all their boats together. All able-bodied men, except the archers, would be taken on in small batches and then landed at the top of the peninsula behind the army of Bougie. The situation would right away be reversed: the enemy would be caught as if in a trap; on one flank he would be pushed back by our archers' arrows, and on the other he would be forced in the direction of the sea, toward which he would go slowly but surely, and would come up against our position behind several barricades of camels. There would be a lovely massacre . . .

The plan was an attractive one; we had such confidence in al-Kahin, and such a need to hope, that our spirits rose. In the next few days the camp saw its earlier enthusiasm reborn in the preparations for the maritime expedition. Everyone was singing again as we honed our weapons and made ready the boats. The men soon began getting on board those minute but innumerable craft. It was then that there loomed on the horizon a galley, a real man-of-war. There could be no doubt that it was an enemy ship, dispatched there to bar our exit by the sea. We were trapped between a powerful army descending on us as fast as its soldiers' legs could carry them, and that fearsome vessel, which would unload more troops when needed and against which our fishing craft seemed paltry indeed.

The situation was getting critical again. I have never admired al-Kahin as much as during those difficult moments. Like any true warrior, far from being overwhelmed by a stroke of bad luck, he was stimulated to use his ingenuity. He stopped drinking completely. After a renewed outburst of anger in which he challenged fate and humanity, and which seemed to give him relief, he once again hit on the right counterstroke. By good fortune we had among our various boats a large fishing *bilancella* of heavy elegance and rounded belly, but with the unexpected suppleness of the fat, allowing it to veer pretty fast under full sail. Al-Kahin ordered us to take advantage of night to fill it with resolute men, whose mission was to hide in it until it was close enough to the enemy vessel for them to attempt boarding. We waited for night with anxious, restrained excitement; then the best fighting men of the entire army entered the *bilancella*. The rest of the night was spent carefully putting the finishing touches to our preparations. All the next day, everyone avoided looking at the enormous fishing boat, which carried our last hopes in its flanks. When nightfall came again, our phony fishermen drifted slowly, as if going out for a catch, toward the mouth of the gulf, where their apparently peaceful prey lay.

With our hearts beating, but silent and motionless, we watched through the openings in our tents the *bilancella*'s progress. The weather was uncertain, a storm perhaps brewing. The sky went gray, drained of its light, which concentrated itself in our orange and white sailing boat. Everything appeared to be going excellently; the enemy galley was probably making preparations for sleep, unheedful as it was of the ponderous course of that peaceable craft, carrying out its prosaic task for the people of the coast. Soon the *bilancella* was only a few cubits away from its fearful foe: catching our breath, we were waiting for the moment when we would hear our soldiers shouting their boarding cry and see them leaping, hatchet in hand; when suddenly hundreds of flames burst forth before our eyes, streaking the violet dusk and crossing the small space between the enemy ship and ours, piercing the *bilancella*. Those cries that we were expecting from our soldiers, it was we who shouted them first—cries of amazement, fear, and rage—followed, alas, by those of our hapless warriors. One enormous fire now rose from the *bilancella*, from which there emerged poor creatures transformed into flaming torches that hurled themselves into the sea, or were shot down by the Bougians' arrows.

It was our first great calamity, the most terrible and the most decisive. Standing on the shore, without hiding ourselves any more, we watched all those men being destroyed and burned, who only a few hours before had been so alive, so spirited, and with hearts full of desire to conquer for their people's freedom. Many among us, clenching our fists and shamelessly letting the tears roll down our cheeks, wondered with disgust why Providence was thus making mock of such a just cause. In its last convulsion, the *bilancella* burst into flame all over in a single blaze, settled on its side, and sank with amazing speed. Soon afterward, nothing remained of all those lives and human industry but some blackened spars with vague tatters of sail hanging, and a few bodies, being patiently brought back by the sea's soothing caress.

Al-Kahin's Death

Finally, al-Kahin agreed to order a retreat. It was high time; we killed a small group of enemy horsemen, who must have reached us by forced march; the bulk of them could not be very far away now. Our leader decided to destroy everything as we passed; our pursuers, too numerous to refrain from living off the land, would be hampered in their advance. There was grumbling in our allies' ranks and for the first time they did not want to listen to him. One can ask anything of a people of farmers except that they cut down their trees and kill their flocks. The order was executed so sparingly that it seemed that they wanted to give the enemy time to arrive and save the wealth, even though he was going to use it, in large part, himself. The inhabitants of the plains do not have the same instinctive faith in their freedom; they prefer being subject to the conqueror's yoke and keeping their riches, rather than living free and poor. The furious al-Kahin tried to punish the peasants; all he had to do for that purpose was to relax the strict discipline of his mountain people, who have always despised the plains folk, and periodically harry them.

That was his second mistake. The mountain people began to harass the farmers again and the farmers to hate their former plunderers. Through anger and disillusionment, some farmers may have lent a hand to the Bougians; in any case, they were suspected of it and treated as if they had. A few excesses occurred, and were exaggerated out of all proportion by fear and hatred. It was said that our soldiers gouged out the eyes of the prisoners or castrated them, then released them in the countryside mad with pain and shame; or, making them kneel in a line, without letting them say a prayer, with a single blow of the knife cut their throats, in which the cry was cut short; that from the slashed wombs of the women, they tore out slowly gesticulating fetuses and then squashed them under their heels. At first we let the rumors circulate since they made us feared and apparently stronger. And it is these excesses, partly imaginary, that historians have recorded; if we are to believe them, our epic story was nothing but a series of horrors. But where can one find soldiers, under somewhat relaxed discipline due to the disorderliness of retreat, who have not indulged in some irregularities? Only what fails in preserving power is called excess. If by this collective punishment of the farmers al-Kahin had brought them to submission, would he not have gone down in posterity all the greater as a military leader?

When he grasped the consequences of that measure, al-Kahin cancelled it; he again severely forbade his mountain folk to act harshly. It was too late; one cannot so easily recapture unleashed lions. The farmers interpreted this as weakness, which it was. Instead of calming down, the country rose up against us. Those who remained loyal to us did so out of fear of being treated as adversaries; and we had hardly passed by when revolt burst out again after us, as wheat springs up again after the passage of horsemen. It was our turn now to experience bitterly the difference between proceeding through friendly and enemy country, where each night was heavy with treachery and the look of each woman and child full of irony and curses. We, the fighters for liberty, were becoming its destroyers, and the Bougians its defenders! All the things that when we were winning had pleaded in our favor, became the proof of our infamy and were held against us. It was during that retreat, as the enemy grazed our horses' tails, when we spent more time in the saddle than at rest, that I was hit by an arrow; I never found out whether it came from the Bougians or from our friends of the day before. It gave me a shoulder wound that I thought would kill me, but it turned out not to be serious. Despite Younous's care, though, it made me suffer terribly.

As misfortune is greedy, it was also at that unhappy time that sad news reached me from Castile. Pedro the Cruel had died and his kingdom had collapsed around him in serious disorder. Dolores had not held up well under all these blows; her face had wrinkled and her hair whitened. Although I tried, I couldn't imagine Dolores grown old. But I had to believe it: when we ourselves age, doesn't the whole world age with us? I myself had changed quite a bit, too. Dolores, my beautiful beloved, must have become only a faded rose on a heap of ruins.

Finally the reply from Damascus arrived. Or, more precisely, they brought us the body of a man who had been killed by an overly nervous sentinel. He had been glimpsed hiding in the bushes; when the guards summoned him, he began to run away, and so he was shot down. Before he died he managed to murmur that he had come from Damascus; the guards then thought that this might be a matter of interest for their leaders. In fact, we recognized him as the servant of our ambassador. He had another nasty wound that he did not owe to our archers. So this poor wretch had galloped across two continents, escaped from a thousand dangers, eluded the snares of vigilant enemies, withstood the effects of a wound that could have killed stronger men than him, and overcome frequent despair that could have killed braver than him. He might have died from a snake bite, a scorpion's sting, or water fever; but no, he had to get himself killed on the very day when he reached his goal. It is useless to scrutinize the designs of Providence and the ends of men.

We never knew what the precise message from Damascus was. Once or twice, the Zenatas had obtained some secret encouragement from Damascus, if not aid. Naturally, this was when the vizier of Damascus considered it useful to make trouble for the established powers of the region. Was it so this time? Or did Damascus consider us already lost? Or had they caught wind of the shameful rumors going around about us? If that were so, one can imagine the fate of our ambassador. Dealt with as the envoy of brigands, the poor man must have been tortured and put to death.

We were beginning to run short of arms. For some time already, we had not been receiving any. Formerly, they were sent to us by various enemies of Bougia who had an interest in seeing its power weakened. Now everyone considered that our struggle was in vain. We ourselves knew deep down that we were heading for disaster. We still sang the poems of Tacpharinas announcing al-Kahin's coming coronation, our glory among the nations, and our future domestic happiness. But we now knew that that kingdom of bliss would remain a dream; that our real lot would be in the end misfortune and death, as the assassinated poet had predicted. Since we were not receiving recruits, we were no longer making good our losses. Even our companions of longest standing, feeling trapped in a hostile country, began to desert. When faithful companions opposed them, the deserters turned their arms against these. A sinister rumor was going around: that we had been betrayed by the son of al-Kahin himself—the one who, in fact, did receive a command with the Bougians. In short, we had no more expectations, and we had nothing to hope for, from God or man.

In the face of this increasing and thenceforth irremediable chaos, our leader did wonders. Once again, he became the great al-Kahin of the hours of glory; and I'm sure that many warriors could benefit from studying our last campaign. But, when fortune has decided to do away with someone, all the stars are against him; what had been his meat becomes his poison. Before, al-Kahin had succeeded in everything he tried; now he was trying all possible tactics, one after the other, and all failed. One day, when we had a fairly large concentration of the enemy before us, he used the camel strategy, usually infallible: either the Bougians had discovered the right response, or our soldiers no longer had any heart to fight, but it almost turned into a disaster.

Al-Kahin finally understood and admitted that he was lost; he ceased imposing his will and again began dreaming every night and talking in his sleep. Once he dreamed that the enemy general was eating the hair on his head; Tacpharinas was no longer there to help him interpret this vision, but its meaning was clear. A few days before, when we were passing through a village, a bird seller's cage had opened on its own; a big blackbird came out and flapped off; then, exhausted by this unaccustomed effort for a prisoner unused to freedom, landed on al-Kahin's head. Everyone laughed to see the bushy crown of our

9. "We followed him out of the camp." Courtesy of Albert Memmi.

leader transformed into a nest; the more impudent advised him to shoo the bird away before he received an egg. There had also been the arrow of a clumsy archer, which had grazed his shoulder; his horse fell on a slope, and had to be put down despite its pleading eyes, bursting with fear. Fate had been multiplying its warnings: it was the end.

The Zenata leader assembled us and announced that since the game was up, he was giving us our freedom. As for himself, his own destiny was ending there. No one said a word. We could have advised him to return to his village, let himself be forgotten, and at least save his life. Perhaps, with time, if his people found new energy . . . But we knew that a man does not leave the stage so easily; our character always pursues us. Al-Kahin was the one who was right: every war is also a war of myths. Since his own had dissolved, he was now no more than the leader of a band, defeated and in flight; even his own folk in the mountains would not want anything to do with him. He asked us if we, his oldest friends, would agree to do him a final service. We trembled, for we guessed what he meant; but we assured him of our complete devotion. Al-Kahin handed over command to the first lieutenant, and we followed him out of the camp. Everyone noticed that his son was not among us.

As we rode slowly behind our leader, Younous told me of Turncoat's death, which occurred while I was on mission to the Burntfaces. At first, Turncoat had not believed that Bologuine would apply the death sentence. Believing that the sovereign, whom he had known for such a long time, and whom so many memories bound to him, only wanted to give him a fright, he remained completely calm. When they came to get him, when he saw the gibbet and the stake for traitors, prepared for him, he understood that he was really going to die. He threw himself to the ground, rolled in the dust, and demanded as a matter of urgency to be taken back to the sovereign, declaring that he had important information to divulge to him. He shouted at the executioners that they ought to remember that he had been the king's friend; if he learned that in this extremity they had prevented him from speaking, he would be most displeased. No one has ever been able to resist Turncoat's persuasiveness; disturbed, the executioners suspended the execution for a moment and took the condemned man back to the palace. Turncoat threw himself at Bologuine's feet and, this time discarding all his noble postures, declared that he was just a poor wretch, a scoundrel twice over, for he had lied twice. He was not only a liar but also a base man: far from having betrayed for his faith, as he had previously maintained, he had accepted Bougian gold. He had even received a large amount, a portion of which he could hand over, if he were released for a moment.

The king listened with amusement to the whole comedy, which Turncoat believed was convincing. Then Bologuine confirmed the sentence, saying that Turncoat was a clown, and it was impossible to know at which moment he had truly lied: Thus, Younous concluded, one always dies as a victim of the character one plays.

While Younous was telling me about this affair, we reached the place still known today, in memory of al-Kahin, as "Wizard's Well," in the center of which is a deep pool, edged with a rim of broad, flat, white stones. It was on this rim that the hero asked to have his throat cut. We did so. At the moment of death al-Kahin murmured: "And now, Lord, it's between you and me!" What did he mean at that final moment? Obviously, that he was going to give account of himself to his Creator; but we understood that he was also going to ask Him to explain Himself. Was he perhaps thinking of the shadows in which God has us live? Or, more simply, of the injustice of his own destiny? The incomprehensible and painful treachery of his son? No one has ever known why the Zenata's son betrayed his father. For gold? Because he was ordered to? Al-Kahin would have given his own life for him: an adopted son, he enjoyed such unstinting love, such anxious care as is rarely given to legitimate children. Why had Turncoat betrayed Bologuine? He had everything: an exalted post, the king's confidence and friendship. What is man, oh Lord? What are we in the Lord's eyes? Nothing, it seems, would have succeeded in quenching the thirst of Turncoat and of al-Kahin's son.

Then, his face keeping the expression of pride which he had had as long as he lived, we sent our leader's severed head to his conqueror. By this we wanted to show our enemy that the battle was over. He was intelligent and generous enough not to push his advantage. We dismissed what remained of the army; the mountain people went back to their mountains and the peasants to their fields. I took leave of my last-remaining comrades.

I had not only failed to win anything in this foray, but I had also lost in it all vestiges of my wealth and prestige, for allying myself with men who, once defeated, became outlaws and good-for-nothings. That is the rule in war. Poor al-Kahin! The lesson that each human life teaches is a small one, but unique: yours was that neither courage nor virtue can save us, if heaven itself abandons us.

Together with my faithful Younous, who alone remained of my small following, I set out for Fez. Arriving in sight of the city, I took lodging at an inn and, as Bologuine had taught me, sent out a man disguised as a porter to see which way the wind blew. It was lucky that I did. We were woken at dawn to hear that it was the party opposed to our interests that was in power this time. To increase our discomfort, the rumor of our exploits with the Zenatas had traveled as far as Fez and there was a price on our heads. Where could we go? Tunis was still in the hands of the Bougians, Bougia was forbidden to us, and Fez was dangerous; all that remained was Tlemcen, where I knew nobody. I was tired of our lands and of myself, in both body and soul. I would have liked to change continents, if my wound had not been taking too long to heal over. I longed for a complete retirement, which fortune was kind enough to provide me with quite soon.

I promised, Sire, to tell you of the fate of the Zenata: as far as their liberty goes, they never won anything. From their mountain retreats, they continued to claim it, and took up their ancient struggle whenever a new leader arose among them. The Bougians, and then the Tunisians who took power again, adamantly refused to give it to them. Finally, however, peace was made and kept. Do you know what its price was, and what happened to the Zenata? They disappeared. What a laughable idea, believing that war for peoples is the worst of all evils! The Zenata have always preferred war to discomfort or boredom; the kind who can stand war can't stand peace. As eternally conquered folk, the Zenata remained eternal warriors; disarmed by peace, they dissolved among their neighbors.

The Brigands

Old age was coming on, announced by irrefutable signs. I sensed I was getting heavier and losing my breath more quickly; I was prolonging my siestas and, despite cold showers and searing hot drinks, I was returning to alertness more and more slowly; I of all people, so proud of my strong legs, which with a single leap could hoist me onto a horse, preferred using the stirrup. In particular, I experienced more and more frequently that bizarre condition, which would begin in the chest with an unbearable pain; then the world would cease and I would enter the night. Each time, I thought I was dying, but I was wrong about myself: when I awoke the world had not disappeared and I had not lost my life. Each time I merely found myself a little weaker, but very much at ease, as if I had been bled or had slept deeply. My meditative body thenceforth seemed to be expecting some decisive event; except for the brief pain in my heart, and my novice's fear, which I was gradually overcoming, the experience of nothingness was no longer disagreeable to me.

Following the Zenata defeat, in order to take care of my wound, I had taken refuge in the midst of the Meharbians, a community of brigands, real brigands this time. This choice also has been held against me; but in fact what has not been held against me? Though I don't take myself very seriously, I will explain my actions yet again (for the best of men is never good enough to disdain public opinion). I had known their chief, al-Ghoul, for whom I had done a favor, in Bologuine's time; I had persuaded the sovereign to desist from exterminating the brigands—not from humanitarianism, really, but for reasons of politics. The sacrifices we would have had to make for success, if we had succeeded, would have been considerable.

Wouldn't it be more advantageous, I had said to Bologuine, to impose on them an annual tribute in gold and troops, in return for leaving them territory for hunting and pillage? This territory could, moreover, be situated on the edge of the kingdom, one frontier of which would thus be protected. It would be all the worse for anyone who ventured there; they would usually be foreigners unfamiliar with our arrangements.

Granting that my proposal would be convenient, Bologuine gave his consent; al-Ghoul remained profoundly grateful to me. He was an unpolished, uncomplicated man, although he could be quite devious when his business required it. He loved nothing as much as gold and women, and gold even more than women. But who doesn't love gold? And who doesn't enjoy women, even if it is sometimes difficult to admit it? To be sure, al-Ghoul was a leader of brigands, but what people, even the most industrious, does not have a slight resemblance to al-Ghoul's brigands? What people does not wish to enrich itself at the expense of others? Moreover, my new friend had in his favor the best that a king can desire: he was admired by his subjects. With brigands or respectable folk, it's always the same: they idolize whoever likes to fight, and wins. Al-Ghoul was brave to the point of foolhardiness. And he had one virtue which, above all others, goes right to my heart: he was generous without regard for the consequences. When, after the catastrophe of al-Kahin, I fell into such extreme misfortune, and I didn't know where to go for my healing because my latest enemies were so vindictive and powerful, he was the only one who dared receive me. Thus chance decided on my last refuge and, not having cause to regret it, I refuse to speak badly of my hosts.

Of all my small following, no one remained except Younous, by God's grace, my first and last companion; he was all I needed, and that was good. My Circassian girl had disappeared in the confusion of retreat; I missed her but I was not unhappy to be free of such an attachment. I entrusted my daily satisfaction to a young slave of good extraction, who was given me by al-Ghoul. She spoke my language perfectly and I spoke hers; but I hardly exchanged more words with her than with the Circassian. I wonder whether I have ever understood any woman, and even whether a man and a woman can understand each other. It seems to me no more surprising, or regrettable, than that water and fire do not marry, although they are useful to each other. I'm only sorry not to have had sons; but am I really sure that I regret it? A king without subjects, a father without children, perhaps that is the best way to be. I cannot erase from my memory the sorrows of Younous and al-Kahin; a dead son gives much more pain than a living one gives joy. And, in the disorder and night following a battle, haven't I often, like all my companions in arms, made use of a woman captive of whom my memory retains no trace? How many slave girls have I known in the brief desire of one moment, dissipated by pleasure? How many sons, the issue of my seed, though not according to law, may be living around the world? Is it really necessary for me to recognize them, if God and Nature do, and if, with the approval of these, I am assured that I will be perpetuated in my own flesh and blood?

In sum, I had finally acquired some wisdom. In any case, I ardently hoped so; which, I will admit, is not the definitive proof that one has attained it, since all ardor is suspect, even toward virtue. On the other hand, as I used to tell myself, complete prudence would be the neighbor of death; it was good that even this victory was continually under siege.

I had had occasion to tell al-Ghoul of my long-deferred hopes of reconquering my father's kingdom. Without hesitating at all, omitting all the conditions and evasions I had met in the best of my friends, the brigand chief put at my service his own hand and those of all his men, whenever I should resolve to act. That warmed my heart and filled me with melancholy: the first time I was offered help wholeheartedly, fate had it come from an outlaw. Was I going to let brigands loose on my unfortunate native land? I thanked him, and vaguely promised to think about it. In order not to be indebted, I offered my new friend my diplomatic talents, which he accepted eagerly. I had acquired the habit, in approaching any man, of asking myself one initial question: what is his ultimate passion? That has always served me well. For al-Ghoul, it was gold; I decided to have him win some, in order to cultivate his friendship better and to live in more comfort.

Noting that on the whole the brigands were excellent fighters, lacking all fear of suffering and death, and following Bologuine's excellent idea, unexecuted alas, I thought of organizing a temporary hiring out of al-Ghoul's men to sovereigns, for his own profit. Its success was swift and unexpected. Very interested and always avid for mercenaries, they acquired the habit of sending regular emissaries, sometimes holding the rank of ambassador, to me in our outlaw's camp. Apart from the highly profitable side of such commerce, it pleased me not a little to deal with all those princes in complete freedom. Al-Ghoul freely ceded me his prerogatives as long as the gold was coming in. Thus, though I still had not succeeded in regaining my throne, I was reigning in a way over brigands.

From time to time, in order to keep my new friend's respect, even though I had not yet recovered full use of my shoulder, which plagued me on rainy days and warned me of approaching storms, I rode out with them or even went on a raid. All I had to fear was that my sudden, curious memory lapses, due to my other illness, should not occur on horseback; but I trusted my own nature and was not mistaken. As long as I was on an expedition, I never had that sort of weakness, as if my body only abandoned me when I was in a safe place.

My life in al-Ghoul's camp, in short, satisfied me fully. Of course, it did happen that I witnessed deplorable acts; during those occasional expeditions, I saw some horrible things, but one does not join company with brigands to contemplate exhibitions of kindness. Moreover, although for respectable people brigands evoke the cruel appetite of instincts beyond all law, this is only partially true. At their work my companions were brutal, speedy, crafty, and indulgent toward their own desires, but they showed themselves trustworthy and ready to give up their lives for anyone whom they considered their friend or associate, even temporarily. Until then I had lived among princes and their highest servants, ministers, and diplomats, who were not openly unjust and apparently respected a multitude of rules. But, as soon as they could do so with impunity, they forgot the word they had given and the treaties they had formally signed, and did not hesitate to betray their ally of the day before or to send entire peoples to their death if they considered it in their own interest. Between the snakes and the wolves, I was not sure that I did not prefer the wolves.

One evening I was brought Younous' body and severed head. He had decided, without me for once, to take part in a small expedition. He no longer had his agility and his eyes deceived him; it was I who now discreetly protected him. His severed head was still grimacing with terror and his lips looked as if they had moved after the fatal stroke. What last truth had he tried to reveal? Had he wanted to warn me about this last test, that terrible, brief moment when the body and head are separated, while the soul flees? I was surprised at myself for not suffering enormously from that misfortune, which deprived me of the only father I have ever known. But no doubt Younous himself would not have wanted me to behave otherwise.

I was preparing to organize the last rites owed to a father by his son, when I had the most unexpected meeting of my life: they came to tell me that a certain black man was asking for me. His face seemed not entirely unknown to me. I had never seen him before, though. He was well dressed, though in the manner of the blacks, in which red and blue predominate. He greeted me and said simply:

"I am the son of Younous."

He added that he had come to ensure that his father had a worthy burial. He did not doubt that I had provided for it, but he thought it was his duty to tell me.

I asked him if he had known for long that his father was living with me in the Meharbians' camp.

"Yes," he said.

And about the other side of it:

Did Younous know where his son was?

"I don't know."

Why all this mysteriousness? Why had he not shown himself earlier to his father? If Younous knew of this son's existence, why had he done nothing to be reunited? Why hadn't he ever said anything to me about him?

When I insisted, Younous's son provided me with the elements missing for me to understand his father's story: Younous had refused to be the sorcerer-prince. It was a serious crime: the dishonor of it involved his whole clan, as I had learned in the land of the Burntfaces. The son never again saw his father, who, moreover, was obliged to leave his country forever. That was not in accord with what the old man had told me, and he had heard what he knew from the lips of Younous himself. That story put my friend in a good light; but the other version was to the son's advantage, since it made him a fallen royal heir. Who was right, Younous or his son? The Lord alone knows the truth. I tried to depict to the person with whom I was talking the constant wisdom of Younous, his unselfishness, his total devotion to me. I told him that whatever happened, I would refuse to condemn my adoptive father. This seemed to make little impression on him. Before we separated, without expecting to see each other again, I asked him his name: he gave me it reluctantly: "Tartour." I remember that Younous had once called me by that name several times over. Obviously, I did not answer right away, since I did not know that he was addressing me. When he realized his error, he apologized; but I could not get him to tell me why he had called me that.

Another day, almost blushing, al-Ghoul entrusted me with a supreme task: he wanted to be recognized as king by the neighboring monarchs. For that purpose he would agree to pay them tribute, though he was more powerful than most of them. That made me smile at first, and then reflect: what had our first ancestor, Yarmoracen, the first king to be crowned, in fact been? What was my father, what was my uncle, if not adoptive kings? Which king was not so? One only had to go far enough back in the past. I reached the conclusion that it would be legitimate to have the brigands' chief crowned king, and I began the necessary steps.

While waiting, I was living in that reddish dustbowl chosen by al-Ghoul for his camp, accessible only by a single path easily defended by a few archers against the most formidable of armies. The countryside was imposing and lovely enough to be worthy of a higher destiny; it satisfied the senses and fulfilled the soul; one had to be tortured by some obsessive care to dream of leaving it. It was the other face of the great lesson of the desert: though the entire earth may belong to whoever dares conquer it, a minute portion is enough for whoever knows how to enjoy it. I had traveled sufficiently to know by experience I could rest my head anywhere. In those couple of acres of beaten earth, open to the sky, where I could meditate, sleep, and stretch my legs, I would have been quite happy to wait for death.

I sincerely believed that it would be so. As soon as I arrived, to indicate I was permanently settling there, I elaborately traced out God's name and fixed it to the best wall of my tent. Of course, I reflected, I had not had my own palace built, as Idris III and Bologuine had done. But, as I told myself in consolation, my few writings would perhaps win me a surer place. Writing is the sister of architecture and is destined to last longer. It was seldom that a whole day passed without my sitting down at my portable writing desk. And since, despite my age, I was praying much less, I concluded that writing must also be a form of prayer.

Also by habit, I continued sketching the novel clothes, arms, and implements I encountered. I no longer expected them to be useful one day; I enjoyed reproducing them for the simple pleasure of their form or the ingeniousness of their making. At last, in that absence of desire, that calm distancing of all self-interest, I asked myself sometimes whether, despite so many adventures, I had not been dreaming all my life, even whether the Kingdom of Within had existed. Then I had to repeat to myself, as one pinches oneself to find out whether one is really awake, that I had been born there, had lived there, and knew its people and customs: my chronicle would prove it if necessary.

Occasionally also I went down to Al-Arish, a neighboring village existing in perfect symbiosis with the Meharbians: in exchange for a little gold and armed protection, providing them with the small items of which they had need. Since I no longer had to live up to appearances, it did not displease me to walk among these simple folk,

10. "I elaborately traced out God's name." Courtesy of Albert Memmi.

gardeners and artisans, whose way of life plunged me on some days into thoughtful amazement: how could they work like that, without respite, begetting children and then dying, leaving to their descendants the same existence? Then I had to admit that we, the favorites of fortune who, in order to cheat the same emptiness and fatal end, rush in pursuit of vain glory, were hardly any wiser than they.

There I go talking about death again, and I can see how much room it has taken up in this story. Death is always here, Sire; it is not we who make room for it. When we are young and strong we can pretend not to see this guest, who is always in the way, but sooner or later it shows up and ends by taking over the whole place. Soon we are obliged to leave the scene and everything goes on as if we had never even existed.

It must not have been written, though, that I had arrived at the last stage of my wandering. It was in this retreat that the message from my cousin the king reached me, authorizing me to return and granting his pardon, for a crime which, of course, I had never committed. A strange letter from Sebbagh, our historiographer, accompanied the king's, testifying to the monarch's good intentions toward me. He added with embarrassment that despite his fidelity to our family, he had never himself been bothered. Through old age or fatigue, a certain gratitude also, he was seeking reconciliation.

To tell the truth, I no longer needed his guarantee. In the depths of my heart, I had admitted for a long time that my cousin was not the monster that I had depicted in my self-interested dreaming, nor even a bad king. He had done his job well and earned his subjects' respect; we, my father and myself, were all but forgotten. Ought I to persevere in a hostile stance that threatened to harm our people? Moreover, news from abroad was far from favorable; new conquerors were arising on the horizon, among whom, you, Sire, were the most formidable. Was I to add to the probable difficulties our state would have?

I even asked myself whether I still wanted to be king, whether I had really ever had that ambition. My destiny had been a long wandering. I had thought I was seeking allies; but I had considered Jonkey too weak, Idris III too powerful, Bologuine too selfish, and al-Ghoul not respectable enough. Perhaps I simply did not want to owe anything to anybody. Had I made a serious attempt to take back my father's kingdom? Hadn't I behaved as though the only kingdom to be conquered was that of myself? In my ultimate wisdom or supreme illusion, I only desired one thing now: to be buried in my native land. In short, my cousin's gesture seemed to me a providential one and I agreed joyfully.

Nevertheless, out of pride, I asked for a period of reflection. I also needed to question Younous; I had acquired the habit of talking to myself while addressing the shade of my dead friend.

"Oh, Younous," I asked him, "Were you teaching me to live or preparing me to die? Is that your secret?"

Younous's shade would not have been his if it had answered me. If I had insisted, it would have reminded me severely of his teaching: "Only ask the questions you can answer yourself. And in order to do that, you have need of nobody. You know as much now about your own death and your own life as any man can know."

I announced my decision to al-Ghoul, who greatly regretted it. He had grown used to seeing me take care of his most difficult affairs, but he did not do anything to keep me against my will. I promised him that I would conclude, from far away, the discussions which had begun about his coronation. He pretended to believe me and embraced me; the brigand's sensitivity affected me deeply. He even offered me a portion of gold, which I accepted so as not to displease him and so as not to go home with empty hands. Finally, the moment to leave arrived. Many of the brigands were weeping, including their chief, and I could not hold back my tears. But I had to leave those good fellows; I spurred on my horse's flanks and went off at a trot. They shouted:

"Come back and live with us again! Don't forget that we are the only ones who know how to bury the dead properly! Only with us will you be preserved to eternity . . .

That amused me, despite my sadness. I had already heard the same claim from other peoples; each one takes pride in whatever he believes most precious. I took fortitude in the discovery that had surprised me so much when I had first made it: each people believes itself to be the best, the most skillful, and the most beloved of God. And I as well, I thought to myself—hadn't I believed myself unique in my own eyes? Oh, Younous, you wanted me to become a prince before I became a king: may God only grant that I have grown worthy of it.

The Termites

Or, al-Mammi's Reply, at Last, to Tamerlane

The rest is known to all the historians.

I was not to enjoy for long that return to which I had so looked forward: it only took a few weeks for me to sniff the smell of the corpse beneath the apparently flourishing flesh of my people. I spoke out: our unfortunate state would not be able to hold out against the new aggressors. People mocked me; they asked me for proofs, which I could not provide. No one can see the termites at work; one needs the ear of a nomad accustomed to the complete silence of the desert, in order to hear the continuous gnawing of death. This time it was my own nation, my own flesh and blood that was involved. Did I have to go back just in order to witness those death throes? Alas, love of one's native land is a part of one's faith; the native land is neither Tunis, nor Fez, nor Tlemcen; the native land is Paradise.

I proposed to the king that I speedily prepare the chronicle of the kingdom and make an inventory of the past. He was mistrustful, thinking I would get revenge for so long a humiliation—by the pen, if not by the sword.

Nevertheless, I set to work, if only for myself. Already, in that semi-retreat among the nomads, I had dreamed of such a task. How I love them, those books into which the author throws his whole self! They are the books in which the author himself is revealed, but the only true books, the only books that enrich a library. What a strange impression it is to go back in time like that! As if one were preparing one's last bed for a long rest at the headspring of life!

I had maps of the country drawn up, I enumerated the tribes and attempted to distinguish genealogies; I collected popular illustrations, the sayings of our wise men, and the guessing games and riddles of our artisans; I sketched our kitchen utensils and noted the best recipes, everyday clothes and those for ceremonies; I listened to magistrates, lawyers, doctors, and, above all, hastened to question the old folk, for every old man's death is a library burning and disappearing forever . . . I had been making acceptable progress in my enterprise, when finally you arose and sealed our destiny.

I was obliged to leave for new adventures.

Hardly had I established myself in Damascus and gone back to my notes, than you reached me again. Here I am at your mercy once more. My life is at its end, my nation has disappeared, and my sorrow leads me astray. I already rely more on my dreams than on my memories. I have to give myself up to sleep to question my friends who have passed on, I have to close my eyes to recapture the smells and taste of fruit.

Now it depends on you alone, Sire, whether I finish my task or not; it will be the first project I have seen through to its end. I will prepare a list of the dead cities: how Cheliff and Casr-Adji, Al-Khadra and Mersa-Djeddadj, Basra, Dai, and Tameddult disappeared; no longer is the rooster's cry heard there, not a single lighted hearth is seen. Without me, who will find the traces of Achir, Tiaret, Al-Batha, or Archghoul? Without me, when the time comes, will my country even have a name?

You asked me two questions. What is the secret of such a rapid collapse of the Kingdom of Within? And what advice can be drawn from it for your future capital, Balkh?

In exchange for the mercy that I ask of you, here are my replies—although, out of ten words, nine are useless (as my teacher, Younous, used to say!); and you already know the most important part.

There is no secret about our downfall, Sire. Without wishing to detract from your great merit, for no one more appreciates your glory than I, we really did not put up a fight. We still bore in our grasp the tall lances of the great nomads; but did we still know how to use them? Oh, how far we had gone from Yarmoracen! How we had forgotten the lessons of the Ancestor!

When he was fighting against the sons of Aktir, his enemies captured his three chief lieutenants; then, in order to wound his courage, sent him the heads of those poor wretches. What did the Ancestor do?

In the presence of the enemy's envoy waiting for a reply, Yarmoracen ordered that the large stones used to hold the stewpot for his tent over the fire be replaced by the heads.

After the last battle with Ghomar, the latter was found at the foot of a precipice, seriously wounded and abandoned by his people. What did the Ancestor do? He decided to have Ghomar skinned alive. The doctors, having probed the victim's wounds, told Yarmoracen that he would have to hurry if he wished Ghomar to perish at his hand. Yarmoracen gave the order to begin immediately, but when they reached the navel the wounded man breathed his last. What did the Ancestor do, since his thirst for vengeance was not quite quenched?

He ordered his enemy's skin to be stuffed with straw and then put in a cage to serve as the plaything of two monkeys that had been raised for this purpose.

When we arrived from the East, borne by our camels led by the Founder's father, my grandfather's grandfather, for a long time we were the only ones who knew how to cross the desert, until we made a gift to the entire continent of this formidable mount. We were appearing in the West all the way to the ocean and in the south to the Black Country, and along our way many peoples perished and were cut off by our swords. We fought against the sea-peoples, from whom, in order to do battle with them, we borrowed their iron chariots. We conquered Sijilmasa, the key to the Bambouc region, the Golden Gate, thrice over; the last time, we kept it permanently, and since then we have not lacked for wealth. The column recording our exploits is luckily still standing. We could have occupied the loveliest cities; we could have put our flocks to pasture forever; but the

Founder's father would never allow his people to abandon its tents. He knew from experience how empires are born in the shade of lances; he sensed in advance how tribes die—by settling down. Our people, he affirmed, is the oldest one on earth; only blood and blood ties must count for us; we are the sons of our fathers and the fathers of our sons; that must suffice us until the end of time.

When the Founder, who was the grandfather of my father's father, arrived leading his camel drivers in the land which was to be ours, the settled folk of the place, frightened by the spectacle of great Bedouins, and noble and fierce beasts, hastened to bring him all the presents that touch the nomad's heart: jars of milk, lambs, female camels, and dates. The Founder laughed with his men at the servile haste of the settled folk; then they drank and ate the provisions all night. But in the morning, he and his men pulled up the tent poles and lances vigorously planted in the earth as is the custom in the desert, and rushed on across the steppes. For, as the Founder used to say, "Whoever has lived in his mountains still abides there; whoever has lived in silk can no longer ride a horse."

Alas, when the fathers grew old, the sons desired rest.

Years later, when he passed by the same spot while tending the flocks, the Founder's son was surprised to find there a forest of young saplings. He asked the settled folk about it: it was actually the result of his father's last camp; the date stones, thrown far off into the night, had rolled into the holes made by the lances and germinated there. He saw a sign from destiny in that, and the Founder's son decided to build his capital there. That is how the palm groves of Gurara were born, in the Year of the Elephant. The site was a good one. A continuously living spring flowed from the middle of the future city, making it possible to resist any siege. The entire country was an island bordered to the north by the sea, to the south by the desert, more impassable than the water for anyone but nomads. We made it into a garden, but soon we were its prisoners.

We were not able to avoid any of the temptations of settled people; who could have done so? In addition to palm, lemon, and orange trees, we had brought from afar for the pleasure of the eyes the aloe with its cascading audacity, the cactus with its bovine grace, and the bougainvillea, whose wild splendor and infinite shades adorn so many walls in so many cities. Now, alas, you know our opulent temples, to which successive kings have added, and all those haughty palaces, which each family insisted on building in order to mark its place well, embellish the capital and express its gratitude to the country we shared. Then, in a moment of ridiculous foolishness, we offered peace to all our neighbors; as if so much wealth would not, on the contrary, draw down on us the perilous envy of all the peoples on earth! You yourself, Sire, if you will pardon me, were you not dazzled by it, to our misfortune?

In short, we were too happy. Our children were beautiful; our boys irritated our neighbors through the insolence of their young lives; our daughters were celebrated and were sought by all around the sea and even beyond the desert. Our artists had known for so long the secrets of melted wax, of polishing stones of *eygriss*, jade, and *calcedonia*, that they had grown weary of their own skills and were again beginning to imitate more barbaric peoples. Our institutions were among the most reasonable on earth, so we were dreaming of foolishness. We had undertaken everything, completed everything, and succeeded in everything.

It was then that you crossed our frontiers without any warning—like a great nomad. Your fame had preceded you; the whole universe feared your name and proclaimed your exploits. But we had long known that our hour was at hand. Our wealth was yours before you had even thought of taking it; we were expecting you. For too long a time, we had not even made war: our people blushed when tents and nomads were mentioned. Times had really changed: there had been water in abundance and shade for so long, that our people no longer wanted to remember that the shade was the shade of lances and the water was won by the great camel drivers.

The king decided on a mass levy of troops, but it was just an empty wish. Your advance guard was reaching the first watch towers, while the council was still arguing about the salt tax.

I myself, I must admit, was a supporter of not even beginning to fight, and of putting ourselves at the mercy of the conqueror: in my heart of hearts, I knew we were destined for massacre. The life of a people is only a long conquest of itself; when it reaches its end, all it has to do is die.

But it is always a mistake to speak one's mind: people murmured about me; they brought up again the old accusation of treachery. I had lived elsewhere for too long; I was now only a foreigner, who no longer had a sense of the land. If it had not been for my relationship to the king, I would have been punished for my outspokenness.

Before the battle, I asked my cousin's permission to leave the country, and it was given me scornfully. In order to keep one's land, should one lose one's life? I was thus able to save myself and save this chronicle, which is all that survives of my unfortunate nation.

Sire, you have paid me the additional honor of consulting me on the subject of Balkh: should you make it your capital? Can one really counsel a king? Would you hear me out if I tried to dissuade you from Balkh? Rather, I will tell you one last story:

One of our sovereigns, who for a long time had been without descendants, finally found that heaven had granted him a son. You may guess his joy at this renewed hope of long posterity. Alas, when he had the young prince's horoscope prepared, as was the custom, he received the reply that the prince was to die young from a scorpion's sting.

After a moment of dejection, however, the king decided to cheat destiny. He had a palace built entirely of glass, where even the most commonplace objects were of the same transparent material, so that no creature, not even the smallest, could crawl there without being noticed immediately.

And for years the prince lived in it, so perfectly protected that it seemed as if the dismal prediction was permanently proved wrong.

Now one day, a poor old woman passed by, asking for alms in such a miserable fashion that the young prince, despite his father's having expressly forbidden it, ordered the beggar woman to be brought inside the palace. Such is the foolish waywardness of youth that it will risk its life for a mere surge of pity.

So the old woman ate and drank until she was full; then, chatting with the prince, she evoked the memory of the origins of his confinement. The lad admitted that since he had never seen a scorpion, he could not even imagine the terrible creature. Not knowing how to describe it to him, the beggar woman went and brought a piece of dough from the kitchen and, shaping it skillfully, made a little scorpion of it.

No sooner had she finished her work when the creature came to life and stung the prince, who fell down dead.

My wisdom may seem to you to be of a sad sort; is there any other kind? What wisdom is not sad? I have seen too many lusty lives cut off, so much pride end wretchedly. I have told you of the disorder into which Fez sank after my departure; but have you heard what fate its first king met? Idris the Great, whose immortal glory it was to found that famous city, choked to death while eating grapes; in order not to tarnish his memory, his ridiculous end had to be concealed from the people. Senchar, another illustrious king of our regions, knew no limits to his pride. In order to build his palace, he brought the most famous artisans from all corners of the world; then, so that no one could make such a monument again, he would have their eyes gouged out; that king drowned to death in his bath.

Shall I also tell you the story of Hamou, the best of our kings, who with his own hands set up the trap in which his own dynasty was to be extinguished?

Out of magnanimity, he insisted on installing in the palace not only the members of his closest family but all his relatives, even the most distant. Anyone who had any relationship to the king was invited to share in his happiness and thenceforth knew no want. Do you know what the result of so much kindness was?

When the great plague broke out, the terrible affliction found assembled under one roof all the living relatives of the king, whether close or distant. Death carried off all of them, large and small.

Hamou was on a pilgrimage at the time. Crazed with sorrow and regret, he hastened back; but, overwhelmed by it all, he died on the way. They searched the entire kingdom for some distant forgotten cousin who could be put on the throne. There was none, and it was necessary to decide on a change of dynasties.

And what of Bologuine, my friend! What of al-Kahin, the hero of an entire people! And even the inoffensive fat king of Tunis! What can I say of so many princes, generous, courageous, and constant, of whom I have known many, killed with sword in hand? Not to mention all those more modest destinies—viziers, ministers, officials—which ended in the same way, their heads cut off, their goods confiscated; a fall as deep as their elevation had been high; and obscurity for their descendants, who keep a silent rebellion in their hearts, and nostalgia for their family's fleeting glory.

How can my own story be summed up, finally, except as a succession of misfortunes in which I have always lost everything, always had to flee just to save my life?

Sire, you have conquered Balkh, and you want to make it your capital.

May it be then the legitimate witness to your power, but stay there only long enough to take care of the wounded, renew your army, and levy taxes. Let the pleasures you take in it be violent but brief. When the nomad who has arisen swoops down on the country, he must enjoy it until he is satiated. But afterwards he must be able to leave and once more sharpen his energies in the contest with the desert. He who settles down will die, though the dying take never so long. Sire, don't ever abandon your tents and your horses.

As for what comes after: fate may spare you longer than the others, but in the end it spares no one. Peoples believe that they ascend from glory to glory, while they go down from stage to stage to nothingness.

It is at the moment when they reach the height of glory that they begin their descent into the tomb. So, as at a spectacle, one can always ask whose turn it is to think he is triumphing, and whose turn it is to begin dying. For death alone triumphs in the end.

What Historians Add

Patient Reader (for so you are since you have borne with me until now), I must bring this story to a close, at least for the time being.

We can take it up again someday, if I have the leisure again and some strength left. Then I will tell you the rest of the adventures of my ancestor Jubair Wali al-Mammi; and perhaps what happened to his descendants, my more recent forebears—the noble Memmi Ettounsi, who was vizier of the king of Bardo, or Lippo Memmi, the famous painter mentioned in the Great Encyclopedia; or again the life of the sage Makhlouf, with which I regaled you in The Scorpion*—but God alone is the master of time.*

While we are waiting, would you like to know whether Tamerlane allowed Jubair to finish his work?

The answer is that he did.

Enthralled by the speaker's intelligence, the sovereign suggested that he should stay in his court and become his historiographer. Jubair refused; he felt he was getting old and preferred to complete the chronicle of his own people. Tamerlane gave him his protection anyway.

Would you like to know whether Tamerlane followed my ancestor's advice?

The answer is that he didn't.

The great conqueror made Balkh his capital.

As for the rest, it's well known; and I'm sure that you're only asking me these questions out of modesty.

Later on, by way of thanking his illustrious conqueror, Jubair offered him a copy of his chronicle; which copy, placed in the library of Balkh, was to be discovered in the ruins of that city.

For Balkh was taken and razed to the ground when its turn came.

Tamerlane, however, did not witness the destruction of his capital. He had died a few years earlier, by curious coincidence in the same year as al-Mammi.

At least that is what some historians think, among them the highly knowledgeable Ayoun. Others, including the most perceptive al-Milli, one of the historiographers of my family, think they have found the traces of my ancestor as the founding sovereign of a new dynasty.

In the absence of decisive evidence, I shall adhere to the second version. I prefer to believe, in fact, that eventually my ancestor, with the aid of his powerful patron, regained the crown that he no longer sought, after having hoped for it for so long.

His judicious renunciation of it was, we remember, the condition under which peace was made with his royal cousin and spoiler. But al-Mammi never ceased to affirm that he would not decline the honor if his turn to reign did come. That may be why his fellow countrymen turned to him.

The ideal monarch is the one who, while not refusing the duty of reigning, nevertheless does not aspire to it; who, having all the qualifications for glory, does not appear to be avidly seeking it.

Our hero won everything in the end, because he no longer claimed anything at all.

Albert Memmi was born in the French protectorate of Tunisia; his first language is Judeo-Arabic. He is the author of a large number of philosophical/sociological essays and is particularly known for his groundbreaking studies of the predicament of the colonized (in *The Colonizer and the Colonized*, 1957), of anti-Semitism and of racism, and for his novels, *Pillar of Salt* (1953), followed by *Strangers* (1955), and *The Scorpion* (1969), all set in Tunisia. *The Desert*, first published in French in 1977, is his fourth novel.

In 1984 President Bourguiba personally bestowed on him membership in the Order of the Tunisian Republic, and in 2004 the Académie Française awarded him the Grand Prix de la Francophonie for his work as a whole.

Judith Roumani is the translator of *Jews in an Arab Land: Libya, 1835–1970*, by Renzo De Felice (1985) and the author of *Albert Memmi* (1987), as well as other studies of Memmi and numerous other publications in comparative literature and Sephardic studies. In addition to being a translator, she is a researcher and writer, freelance lecturer, the director of the Jewish Institute of Pitigliano, and editor of an online quarterly journal, *Sephardic Horizons.*